PENGUIN BOOKS

BORN AND BRED IN MYANMAR: A BOOK OF FIVE SHORT STORIES

Moe Moe Inya was born in Daik-U in 1944. While attending Yangon University in 1964, she began writing poems under her pseudonym from Inya Dorm. She wrote her first novel, *Pyauk thaw lann hmar San ta-war* in 1972 and received the National Literature Award for it in 1974. She also received short novel awards in 1980, 1982 and 1986 for the novel and short novel collections. Her books have been translated into English, Russian, Japanese and Chinese.

Her family owns and runs Sarpaylawka Publishing House, winner of the Lifetime Accomplishment award at the 2020 Publishing Awards in Myanmar.

She worked as the editor of *Sabel Phyu* magazine from 1989 till her death in 1990.

Born and Bred in Myanmar

A Book of Five Short Stories

Moe Moe Inya

Translated by Mra Hninzi

PENGUIN BOOKS
An imprint of Penguin Random House

PENGUIN BOOKS

USA | Canada | UK | Ireland | Australia
New Zealand | India | South Africa | China | Southeast Asia

Penguin Books is part of the Penguin Random House group of companies
whose addresses can be found at global.penguinrandomhouse.com

Published by Penguin Random House SEA Pte Ltd
9, Changi South Street 3, Level 08-01,
Singapore 486361

Penguin
Random House
SEA

First published in Penguin Books by Penguin Random House SEA 2022

ISBN 9789815017113

Typeset in Garamond by MAP Systems, Bangalore, India
Printed at Markono Print Media Pte Ltd, Singapore

www.penguin.sg

This book is a tribute in celebration of Moe Moe Inya's 75th birthday,
which falls on 24 October 2019.

Moe Moe Inya
'Gone but Never Forgotten'

Contents

Khin Soe, Resident of Kin Pun Sakhan, Kyaiktiyo, Mon State

Among their group, Khin Soe was the youngest. He had a tiny body. Even his cousin sister Aye Mya, who was only two years older than him, was taller and bulkier. But among them, Khin Soe was the swiftest and the most light-footed. He was a dapper boy.

'This weighs a total of 32 viss. How many of you are there?' Ko Aung Myint asked the question as he pulled down the steelyard trigger.

'Two.'

'You cannot do this with only two carriers!'

'We can do it.'

'No, no, call another one.'

Khin Soe turned and looked at Aye Mya behind him.

'Just call Aye Hla.'

Aye Mya beckoned Aye Hla who was standing and looking close by. Aye Mya's sister Aye Hla joined them. Ko Aung Myint took one look at Aye Hla and shook his head imperceptibly.

Aye Hla did not appear fit to be a carrier. She had a dark complexion and was way too skinny. Such youngsters were not allowed to carry heavy weights. But the carriers wanted larger shares with fewer persons carrying heavier loads. It could not be helped. A group of three persons, however, was at least acceptable.

Khin Soe briskly pulled down the leather bags from the steelyard. The owner waited and looked at his bags being counted. He made a mental note too. Four big leather bags, one bedroll and one basket.

'Elder brother, are you going up right now?' Khin Soe asked the traveller, who owned the luggage.

'Only after we have had lunch.'

'We will go ahead. You will rest at Yay-Hmyaung-Gyi, will you not? We will wait there. Which rice shop are you putting up at?'

'Whichever shop you want.'

'Then we will wait at Khattar-Lwin. Follow us there, alright?'

'We may even catch up with you along the way. You have heavy loads to carry.'

Khin Soe smiled tantalizingly. 'Just wait and see, Uncle.'

The man patted Khin Soe's shoulder and laughed.

'Well, if you get there first, wait for us. We will climb leisurely. We have old men and women in our group. If you can wait for us, you will be good company.'

'Yes, but during this period, there is no dearth of pilgrims along the way,' Khin Soe replied pertly and looked back at his group. Aye Mya and Aye Hla had already put the luggage into carrier baskets. Khin Soe weighed the three baskets by hand to gauge if the weights were equal. Then, he nimbly lifted up one basket onto his back and pulled down the two handles of the basket to his shoulder. 'Aye Mya and Aye Hla, you two go in front.'

Aye Mya readjusted her *longyi* to make it short and firm. Stout as she was, she could lift up the ten-viss basket onto her shoulder nimbly. Aye Hla was wanly. She was wearing a pair of ragged rubber slippers and her insteps were grimy with tendons showing. Her blackened shin bone seemed to be protruding. But one should not underestimate her frailty. Like the others, she ably lifted the basket onto her back. At first, her body seemed to lurch a little but when they started the climb, she was ahead of everyone. The sleeveless voile blouse she usually wore did not show any hint of perspiration.

Khin Soe followed the two sisters, five minutes after they had left. It was Taboetwe (February) so there was not much heat, but the sunbeams of noon shimmered on the path. After passing by rice shops and bamboo goods shops, it became shady and the pilgrims' climb was now enjoyable.

Khin Soe took slow-and-steady steps on the mountain path to the Kyaiktiyo hair relic Pagoda, which he had climbed countless number of times before.

* * *

'This is such a mystical and almighty pagoda. It is believed that making a pilgrimage here three times will make you rich! I come here once a year.'

Hearing a woman pilgrim chatting through erratic breaths, Khin Soe smiled coyly. Though it was not known whether other pilgrims really got rich, Khin Soe's family could make ends meet because of what Kyaiktiyo's could offer. Before Khin Soe was born, his parents had settled down in the small Kin Pun village. They made their living as farmers, just like others. As the volume of pilgrims to the sacred Kyaiktiyo Pagoda multiplied gradually, the people living around Kyaikto and Kin Pun Sakhan had the opportunity to set up businesses and commercialize them.

Those who had money to invest, opened rice shops and souvenir shops, while those who had physical strength did well in the carrier business. Khin Soe's father himself made money by using his stout and hefty body, so it was no wonder that Khin Soe and his brothers also earned their living in the same way.

Their father supported the whole family by working as a carrier. However, it could not be said that their days of poverty were in the past. Khin Soe's brother was sent to Kyaikto school up to seventh standard. After that, the boy said he wanted to work so he was sent to his uncle in Sittaung. Up till last year, Khin Soe was in school in fourth standard, but unfortunately his father had to be hospitalized because of liver disease. Since the father did not want his younger son to leave school, he sent for the elder brother in Sittaung to return. The boy came back but he was not fit to be a carrier. During the Moke-Gamawt battle, he had received a gunshot wound and had to be hospitalized. Now, he walked with a limp.

So Khin Soe asked his father to wind down and retire, and the boy worked as his substitute. The father kept saying repeatedly that he would send the boy back to school when he had recovered and could work again. But Khin Soe did not consider it a burden to shoulder the responsibility. There were many other youths of the same age at Kin Pun Sakhan who happily went up and down the mountain with heavy loads.

The loads on their backs transformed into cash money, which provided them the subsistence amount for their daily life.

'Oh, I am motivating myself to climb because this is a holy pilgrimage but alas, I am so very tired!' One woman was heard complaining.

The closer one approached the Yay-Hmyaung-Gyi camp, the rougher the ascent was. But the pilgrims climbed with elan and fortitude. Khin Soe climbed steadily, and he walked closely to a group of pilgrims nearby in order to amuse himself.

For Khin Soe, meeting all kinds of pilgrims from all kinds of places was an interesting experience.

'Let us rest for a while.' The woman and, seemingly, her children, a boy and a girl, entered a recreation hut and rested. Khin Soe joined them. He threw down the carrier basket with its contents onto the bamboo bench. He was thirsty but he did not drink. Feeling the cool breeze coming in through the bamboo trees, he sat down on the bench with his legs dangling. The pilgrim family went to the drinking water stand where a sign said '10 pyas per cup' and drank the water they had long been longing for. The girl, who was about Aye Hla's age, gulped down the water until the it overflowed from the edge of her lips and streamed down her sweating neck.

'Daughter, drink slowly. You will choke.' The mother warned the daughter. The girl drank one and a half cups before letting the cup fall through her fair fingers. Her brother took out some coins from his jeans pocket and paid the fee for the water. Then they returned to the bamboo hut and sat on the bench near Khin Soe.

'Ah, oh so tired. Still a long way to go. What a pity!' The girl threw down her little plastic handbag beside her and grumbled. She combed her short hair with her pointy-nailed fingers then shook her head.

'This is only the beginning. Do not grumble,' her brother said.

'What is wrong with grumbling? I say I am tired because I am tired. Are you not tired too?'

'Not at all. No big deal.'

'You are lying. If you are not tired, why do you not go straight up without resting?'

'I can do it but I have to wait for all of you.'

'Do not wait. No need to do so.'

'I am not waiting for you. It is for mother.'

'Nonsense!'

Khin Soe watched the two loving siblings quarrel and found it heart-warming and delightful. At home, Khin Soe had a younger sister called Gyit Tu who was four years old. Gyit Tu was fair, chubby, and cute. He thought to himself, 'When Gyit Tu grows up, she will perhaps be pretty like this girl.' Since the birth of Gyit Tu, his mother had become weak and sickly and was confined to bed. Before that, she carried durians and jengkols in bags and traded them. Now, she could only cook rice and curry for the family.

'Hey, do not keep quarrelling. Let us climb again.' The mother chided them and so the two squabbling siblings held their mother by the hand, one on each side, and continued their climb. Khin Soe lifted his carrier basket onto his back.

'Brother, if you can really can climb all the way up without resting, how about climbing with heavy loads like the boy?' The girl pointed her chin at Khin Soe and teased her brother. The brother changed the position of his small leather sling bag and turned around to look at Khin Soe. Khin Soe's back was bent with the heavy load to overcome the pull of gravity during the ascent but he straightened up a little and smiled at them.

'Of course, I can carry it. Shall I prove it? Young brother, how heavy is the load?'

'About 10 viss.'

The boy shrugged his shoulder. He was wearing canvas shoes, which were now sliding off at the heels with a thudding sound.

'Now you are chicken-hearted, are you not?' The girl laughed mockingly. Their mother looked at Khin Soe with interest.

'Yes really. If we had to climb with such a heavy load, we would be in a fatal situation!'

The girl stroked her hand through her hair and smiled at Khin Soe. 'Are you not tired?'

'Of course, he is tired. No need to ask!' The brother answered. Khin Soe just smiled. He held the two handles of the carrier basket on his shoulder more tightly. Right then he started to feel hungry. That morning because he had to reach the labour office in good time, he had no time to eat his fill. Workers who had registered at the labour office like Khin Soe, had to take turns as carriers but sometimes when someone missed their turn, there could be substitutes and Khin Soe always waited for that chance. The more carrier turns he got, the more he could earn.

'How old are you, Boy?' the woman asked him.

'Thirteen years old, Aunty.' Khin Soe answered respectfully.

The woman looked at the dashing Khin Soe with a pleased look and nodded her head. 'Just think. He is younger than you Son by four years and younger than you Daughter by two years. Working so hard at this age is enviable. You Son, at home, you have never even carried a bucketful of water!' The woman remarked as she looked at her son and daughter. Khin Soe did not know whether to take pride or feel downhearted. He just listened to them happily making conversation with each other and followed them with delight.

'Yes Mother, at home, brother Ko Zaw never helps around the house. He just goes out all the time!' The girl teased her brother again.

'Oh, and you, you just read picture books. You cannot even cook a pot of rice!' the brother retorted.

'Of course, I can cook but I get shouted at by the cook when I enter the kitchen.'

'Of course, she would shout at you. You are useless. The rice you cook becomes sticky rice.'

'Mother, he is talking rubbish.'

'So what if I talk rubbish? See if you can catch up with me!' The brother ran up a rather steep part of the ascent. The girl ran after him. Then, as the mother was shouting 'Hey, hey' the girl slipped and slid down.

'Just imagine! These children of mine! At home they quarrel, while climbing they quarrel, quarrelling all the time for nothing. Show me Daughter, where are you hurt?'

'No pain anywhere Mother. Ko Zaw must be punished for this!'

The brother came back when he saw his sister had fallen down. He took the plastic sling bag from the girl's hand and helped her up. The girl reached out and pounded her brother's back with her fist. The mother shouted at them. 'Come off it, behave well and move up. The cakes for hsoon-offering at dawn have been pressed flat. Such naughty children!'

* * *

Once they entered Yay-Hmyaung-Gyi camp, its cool and refreshing natural vegetation and environment were exhilarating and invigorating.

Aye Mya and her sister were waiting for Khin Soe at the rice shop. If the pilgrims did not mention any shop in particular, they usually went straight to a shop they were familiar with. This way, it was beneficial for them. If the pilgrims did not pay for their food, the shopkeeper fed them free of charge. There were a few pilgrims who were fed out of benevolence. Mostly, they ate the rice packets that they brought with them and if they had no rice packets, they bought their meal for 5 kyats each. But every rice shop let Khin Soe and group eat their fill for 5 kyats out of goodwill.

Khin Soe first went to the water pot and drank his fill. He did not drink on the way up because it would have made his belly full and slowed down his steps. Aye Mya and Aye Hla were resting on the shop's bamboo floor.

'How many persons are there?' the rice shop owner, Daw Yi, asked.

'It's a group of twelve, Aunty. They are well-to-do people. They are sure to buy food from you.'

Daw Yi had the habit of asking if the customers were wealthy and that was why Khin Soe told her before he was asked. Pilgrims who brought a lot of money were ready to spend freely. Photographers also followed such groups.

'But they have already eaten at Kin Pun base camp. They said they will continue to climb after resting a while,' Aye Mya said.

'But they will sleep here on their return,' Khin Soe said.

At that time, some people from Khin Soe's pilgrim group arrived. Khin Soe greeted them briskly and showed them to their tables in the shop. Soon after, the remaining persons arrived and ordered cold drinks and fried venison. Aye Mya and Aye Hla had to carry the leather bags of the women and led them to the bathing spot. Khin Soe took care of the men around the table and waited pertly. All at once, they came to notice Khin Soe.

'Hey boy, come here. What is your name?'

'Khin Soe, Uncle.'

'Good name. Where do you live?'

'I live in Kin Pun Sakhan.'

'How old are you?'

'Thirteen years.'

'You look ten. Do you not go to school?'

'Up till last year I did. But before the fourth standard exam, I had to quit.'

'Is that so? Why?'

'My father became unwell and I had to take his place as a carrier.'

Because of Khin Soe's briskness and sweet disposition, he was usually more favoured than other youngsters. This had earned him a free meal many a time. As for Aye Mya and Aye Hla, they were shy girls and usually sat huddled in a corner. But Khin Soe was generous. If there was something to eat, he usually called his group and shared it with them. And although the sisters were shy ones, they would slog through the food and relish it. Now thanks to Khin Soe, they had fried venison and some snacks.

After resting a while, everyone prepared to continue their climb. Khin Soe was hungry but he ate just enough to appease his hunger and then lifted his carrier basket onto his back and started out first. The mother and her two offspring with whom he had earlier made company had already left, so he did not see them anymore. Khn Soe and the rest climbed up the cool pleasant ravine. Spring water from the hillside drifted along the bamboo troughs. The sound of leaves brushing against each other and the onrush of breeze could be heard distinctly. Some pilgrims descending from the mountain stopped at a natural pond with the sign 'Magic Pond' and drank water from it to appease their thirst. Afterwards, they threw coins into the pond and continued on their way.

Khin Soe tried to make a mental calculation of the number of coins there must be in the pond and then continued his climb.

On the ascent path, there were some people who swept and cleaned the path with a broom, their bowl for donation lying alongside. It was a livelihood through merit-earning. Whatever you may say, it could not be denied that the ascent road had become a smooth plateau due to this activity. 'The access track must be clear, the pilgrim must be healthy, money must be sufficient; only if all three comply, one can come here. It's a rare chance. I am clearing the path by sweeping away the trash and small stones. You may earn merit by donating as much as you desire.'

During the rainy season, there was no pagoda festival because the rains made the ascent path too dangerous for the pilgrims to traverse. But for Khin Soe, it was no time to rest. Only if he worked the whole year round, could his family make ends meet. Last year during the rainy season, his father was still healthy. Father and son used to climb up the mountain and bring betel and jengkol. In the heavy rains, they trembled with cold but Khin Soe enjoyed the adventure. On the mountain, there were plenty of others who made some kind of living there. Khin Soe accepted the fact that it was only natural to make a living at one's native place.

They came to a flight of steep stone stairs. He readjusted his carrier basket, straightened his body, and climbed up step by step.

At the top of the stairs, a group of pilgrims was resting. He saw about ten youths. They looked happy together so Khin Soe thought to himself that they would be good company for him.

'Hey look. This boy is climbing steadily with his carrier basket. You all should at least catch up with him.' One of the group members said as he pointed his finger at Khin Soe.

'No big deal. We are game!' They climbed alongside Khin Soe. From their chatter, Khin Soe learnt that they were students. It was delightful and pleasant to watch them. They were free and easy. They had a fortunate life. Khin Soe did not feel the heavy load on his back but he felt that his life was burdened with family knots.

Khin Soe had no time for leisure at home. When there were pilgrims galore, he was climbing up and down the mountain path.

On nights he got to return home, he ate his fill and went to bed completely frazzled. After giving the carrier fees he had received to his mother, Khin Soe always felt light-hearted and reminisced his childhood. He did not have many playmates. Most boys his age were also working as carriers. As for the girls, if they were not carriers, they went up the mountain to sell culinary goods.

'You are under-average. You each have only one bag and yet you have taken almost four hours. Hurry up and climb.' When the youth, who seemed to be the leader, said that, the three girls in the group were not too happy. Perhaps, they had thought that this pilgrimage would be like an excursion. During the hot season when schools were closed, a lot of students came to the pagoda. People who worked in offices came in groups too. Some continued further to Moulmein after descending from Kyaiktiyo Pagoda. Only when the rainy season approached, did the pilgrims become fewer in number. Then, Khin Soe and other carriers could rest. But the resting was only from carrier work. During this period, they changed their business to selling durians and jengkols in Kyaikto.

'Well, let us not rest too long. We should continue climbing. The girls better go in front.'

The girls looked at one another. The thin girl with brownish complexion was massaging her thigh. 'I wish I could stay behind, May Thu.'

'Do not give up! You should not go back when you have reached this far. It would be a shame. I too am tired. Come, let us do the climbing leisurely.'

The two girls supported each other and continued climbing. The other one, unsmiling, was faltering in her steps.

Then Aye Mya and her sister caught up with the rest of them. Aye Mya bowed slightly so that her yoke inclined forward as she climbed up step by step. Aye Hla, defying her lean body and appearance, climbed straight up unperturbed. Looking at her, you would think she was carrying just a light backpack.

The three girls looked at one another and before their leader could say anything, they continued climbing. Soon, the two sisters overtook them.

Khin Soe mixed with the boys at the back and climbed steadily. The students were talking in amazement about the natural greenery and environment. A new place to visit must surely be full of wonders. To Khin Soe and other carriers, it was no longer a novelty. Instead, the beauty of big cities and towns amazed them.

Khin Soe, who had only been to Kyaikto, had gone to Yangon for a visit the previous year. He got acquainted with a bus driver U Hla Pe, and it was U Hla Pe who took him to Yangon. There, he had to stay at U Hla Pe's place in North Okkalapa. The next day when the bus left for Kin Pun Sakhan again, he returned. Khin Soe did not have the chance to do much sightseeing in the city. While he was in the moving car, he saw high-rise buildings, throngs of people just like at pagoda festivals, and that was all. He paid homage to Shwedagon Pagoda from the car. U Hla Pe consoled him by saying, 'Next time, I will show you around the town leisurely.'

'Khin Soe, you have reached here only now? This time you are so slow!'

Blanket cradle carriers U Nyo and Ko Ba Myaing reached Khin Soe's side, so he made way for them. The person inside the blanket-cradle could not be seen. The sagging cradle was sealed from front to back as a safety measure. Those pilgrims who could not hike up the mountain path had to rely on cradle carriers. Likewise, the carriers relied on such pilgrims for their subsistence. Sometimes, they even encountered laughable situations. If in a group of pilgrims, there was an elderly person, cradle carriers hovered around the group, even if the elderly person claimed that he could make it to the top on his own. Sometimes, halfway through, the old person would give up and the carriers got the job, but sometimes elderly persons with stamina did not even glance at the carriers and made it to the top on their own. That would then mean that the carriers' hike was in vain, and they had to come down empty-handed.

Khin Soe rested together with the student group. That morning he had woken up early but he did not have ample breakfast, so he felt a bit weak. At the rest area when he saw the students buying and eating crispies, his mouth watered. But he had no cash on him. Only when they got to the top, the carrier fee would be settled and it would be divided among the three of them. The fee was 25 kyats per 10 viss so they would be receiving about 80 kyats, which came to about 25 kyats for each of them. And, they would have to buy their own meal up there.

The students were enjoying the crispies leisurely so Khin Soe prepared to go up on his own. One of the three girl students was suffering from dizziness and the others were trying to bring her around. They would take a while before resuming the climb.

Khin Soe lifted his load onto his back and started up with a good foothold. The path was smooth but the small stones were slippery. His worn-out rubber shoes made it difficult to get a firm footing. At that moment, Chit Swe, who was carrying a child in a carrier-basket, caught up with him. Chit Swe was bellowing out songs to make the child happy. The child in the basket was giggling with pleasure.

'Hey child, are you not afraid to ride in this basket? Why do you not cry and holler for me to put you down? If you feel like crying, just cry!' Kin Soe teased the child.

It was not easy to make the ascent carrying a child. Along the way if the child was fussy, Chit Swe had to put the child down and appease him. Now because of Khin Soe's teasing the child was annoyed, so Chit Swe reached out and kicked Khin Soe.

'Hey child, why do you not cry? Or you can piss!' Khin Soe continued teasing the child.

'Hey! Do not do it Khin Soe. Just now I had to coax him and buy him some snacks.'

Khin Soe took pity and stopped his teasing The sun was almost setting.

Khin Soe took brisk steps and continued climbing. He must get to the top before the luggage-owners.

It was the start of the Nagabat ascent.

* * *

What a delicious meal! Although paid for by others, the carriers were not coy about lapping up the food. The five extra servings beside them were emptied in a moment. The luggage owner paid for their food but the shop owner charged only 5 kyats for each serving and nothing for the extras. Otherwise, it would be embarrassing for the carriers.

Aye Hla was the leanest but she ate the most. Pouring gravy on the three rather hard pieces of feather back fish balls, together with fish paste sauce and vegetable side dishes, she ate three whole plates of rice. After the meal, as usual, the two sisters retreated to a corner and sat there quietly. Khin Soe waited on his customers. Soon, 'One moment, Khin Soe' could be heard repeatedly. He was popular with the pilgrims.

On the pagoda platform, a mixture of fog and gentle breeze created a chilly atmosphere. The sound of tinkling pagoda bells was pleasant to hear in the early nocturnal hours. The pilgrims had fallen asleep because of fatigue. Aye Mya and Aye Hla were huddled together in a corner sharing a blanket. Khin Soe, who had ventured out early that morning, had neither brought a blanket nor a sweater. He would feel colder tonight but did not want to pay the 2 kyats rental fee for a blanket. He drew up his pasoe to his head and curled up.

'Hey Khin Soe, do you not have a sweater?' A pilgrim who was already familiar with him asked.

'No, elder brother.'

'Here, put on my jerkin.'

Khin Soe thankfully took the jerkin and put it on. His whole body sank in the warmth of the jerkin, and he slipped into a sleep instantly.

* * *

'Sister, please buy some flowers. I'll give you extra. There are no flowers being sold on the pagoda square. Please buy some from me. Come, Sister. Buy some flowers.'

The voices of the flower sellers were loud and piercing. Sellers from two different shops were shouting over each other so it was confusing to the buyer. The pagoda square was crowded with early dawn hsoon-offering pilgrims. Every footstep on the flagstone made one shiver with cold. The Kyaiktiyo Pagoda, which lacked sunlight at the moment, was majestically perched on a high rock, making it look like it was in imminent danger of toppling over.

The sound of prayers of the pilgrims who had lighted up candles and joss sticks to pay homage to the pagoda was overwhelming. At the top of the pagoda, a holy man was happily receiving gold leaves, jingle bells, and small bells in a decorated chariot that had been hauled up using a pulley system. The pagoda square was fragrant with the abundant aroma of flowers and offerings of cakes, pastries, candies, and fruits were in abundance.

Looking at pilgrims who couldn't get enough of kowtowing and paying homage to this highly inaccessible mighty pagoda somehow gave one a sense of joyful bliss.

Khin Soe sat in a corner and waited for his guests. Usually after paying homage, pilgrims would wander to other areas near the pagoda. When the sun came out, they would take photographs as a souvenir. If they needed a photographer, Khin Soe would contact Ko Nyan Myint, a photographer with whom he was acquainted.

Some pilgrims who had finished paying homage prepared to collect the offering plates and respectfully discarded the offerings.

The resounding wishes, promptly followed by 'sadhu', meaning well-done, repeated three times, reverberated throughout the pagoda square.

* * *

'Buy Shwe Nan Kyin *Thanakha* chunks. They are yellow and smooth. They can cure eczema and pimples. The name was given because Queen Shwe Nan Kyin favoured this genuine thanakha.'

Sellers of Kyaiktiyo products such as thanakha, a variety of herbs and oil balm, were vending their goods in loud voices, trying to make themselves heard by the pilgrims who were quite few at this time.

Khin Soe took the pilgrims to Kyeekanpazat. There, looking at people wishing and throwing coins into the gap between two stones shaped like a crow's mouth, Khin Soe had to stop himself from feeling like a wet blanket, in case he might be damned. He then led the pilgrims to Mote-So-Ma-Taung Pagoda. The pilgrims donated stone slabs which were selling at 3 kyats each. The person collecting donations then gave the slabs to donors who went and personally placed them at the foot of the pagoda.

The sunshine burgeoning from below the mountain rose gradually. The fog thinned down. Now the pilgrims had the chance to behold the shimmering golden pagoda with awe and veneration. Khin Soe dutifully paid homage to the pagoda. Though he was at the pagoda every four days, he never failed to pay homage at any time. He was thankful. It was because of the blessings of this stately pagoda that his family's present situation was financially sound, was it not?

'Do you want to view Yathayt Taung? Or Khamauk Taung? One view will cost 25 pyas. Multiple views cost 50 pyas.'

A person with binoculars was calling out. Pilgrims rushed to view pagodas in far-off hills and mountain ridges.

When they returned from the pagoda square to the rows of rice shops, Khin Soe was beginning to get hungry. From the 25 kyats he had received, he had not spent a pya. He had not even washed his face thoroughly this morning because he did not want to spend on a cup of water which costed 25 pyas. He had washed his face with using the leftover water from others.

When the pilgrims ate, as usual, Khin Soe tended to their needs and waited by their side. 'Why do you not eat too?'

'I am not hungry yet.' Khin Soe gulped his saliva and replied. He had already received his fees so who would feed him now? The two sisters, Aye Mya and Aye Hla, also were quiet with a hungry look. When the pilgrims had finished, there were quite a lot of leftover dishes.

'Hey, Aye Mya and Aye Hla, come here.'

But before he had finished the sentence, the sisters got to the table nimbly. To please the shop owner, they helped collect the empty dishes with enthusiasm. Afterwards, they ordered platefuls of rice and the three of them sat down to eat with relish.

'I will pay for the youngsters too.' The pilgrim said, pointing at Khin Soe and the girls. Khin Soe thought to himself that of all the merits that this person had earned from his good deeds that morning, feeding them would be the most significant one.

* * *

Just as Khin Soe was preparing to trek down again, Ngwe Moung and his sister arrived. They took a look at Khin Soe's luggage and remarked, 'You have quite a lot of luggage. Why do you not share some with us?'

Sometimes, the pilgrims hired carriers only on the way up but not on the way down.

'Why? You have no luggage for the way down? Then you just go down empty-handed. It's my luck to get this luggage.' Khin Soe replied as he put the leather bags in the carrier basket.

'We had no luggage since we climbed up. It is not our turn yet. We came up because some pilgrims who carried their own luggage told us they would most likely hire us on their way down.'

'And now?'

'We have no idea when they went down. We fell asleep.'

Khin Soe laughed though he did not want to. Because of unprincipled travellers, Ngwe Moung and sister had to hike up the mountain needlessly.

'So, you missed a meal too?'

'Yesterday we brought a rice packet.'

'Well then, you can share one luggage.' Khin Soe took pity on fellow carriers and shared his luggage.

But in a way it was good too. The weight they carried the day before was not an easy load. Now the three of them could carry the two carrier baskets in turns.

Aye Mya and Aye Hla lifted the two baskets on their backs. Khin Soe took out one big leather bag from Aye Hla's load and slung it over his shoulder. As for Ngwe Moung and his sister, Ngwe Moung carried the basket and his sister slung the leather bag over her shoulder.

'You wait for us at Yay-Hmyaung-Gyi. And take good care of the luggage. The bags are not locked.'

'Do not worry.'

Workers like Khin Soe, who had registered at the labour office, had to guarantee that there would be no loss of any luggage. If there was any loss, they had to pay indemnity. So, they had to take special care. And supposing there was a loss, it would be quite a burden if the owner claimed 100 kyats for a 50-kyat item.

'Kyaiktiyo souvenirs, Kyaiktiyo souvenirs . . . '

Pilgrims who on their way up were too tired to make purchases, were now happily and heartily buying souvenirs priced at a reasonable price.

Looking downwards at the expanse of territory, it was amazing to see the tracts of mountain that one had covered. Khin Soe and the sisters trekked down together with the luggage-owner pilgrims with whom they had become friendly. In the group, there was a youngster who was of the same age as Khin Soe. But his appearance was not the same. That boy was hefty and cute with a clean look. With his besmirched pants and jacket, his smart look had stood out. He was wearing a slanted, broad-brimmed bamboo hat and made his way down in front, linking hands with a woman who was apparently his grandmother.

'Hey grandson-and-grandmother pair, watch your steps. Descent requires more vigilance than ascent. If your foothold is not secure, you will fall down and roll over.' The older sons and daughters from behind shouted out a warning to them.

'Do not worry. My grandson is reliable. On the way up too, it was he who gave me a helping hand. My grandson's deeds will surely earn him a high standing and long life.' The old woman replied to the others. Then, she muttered wishes of health and happiness incessantly. Seeing the grandson and grandmother made Khin Soe think of his mother. She was not old yet but she was aging and seemed to be in her declining years. Although his mother lived at Kin Pun Sakhan, since the birth of Khin Soe and his siblings, she had never gone up to the Kyaiktiyo Pagoda to pay homage. They only heard her say that she had been there when she was young. In her youth, the mountain path up to the pagoda was arduous, there were not many pilgrims and shops. Sometimes one could even come across wild animals. Khin Soe had frequently been up the mountain but never ever encountered or chanced upon a wild animal. During the festival days, he had gone up with his father to buy betel but they had never affront robbers either. And Khin Soe was not someone to reflect and be scared of things he had not experienced. His courage was comparable with his father's. When his father was hale and hearty, he was a vigorous and sprightly man.

The pilgrims stopped for a while in front of the Shwe Nan Kyin stone statue. They reminisced about the touching story of an afflicted girl. Khin Soe had heard time and again about Shwe Nan Kyin since he was young. But the story about Shwe Nan Kyin told by his mother from the record and the story related in today's books were not quite the same.

The story goes that Shwe Nan Kyin who was crowned queen by the king failed to make a devotional offering to the protector spirit, and so a tiger was set upon her to kill her. Khin Soe was not a modern, educated person but as a young man, he reasoned that it was strange to come across a tiger in a desolate environment. But Khin Soe was truly amazed by the complex construction of the Kyaiktiyo Pagoda.

'If tourists could see this pagoda, they would be amazed. It would be nice if it was more accessible.' One person in their group commented.

'I heard that the engineers are making calculations to build motor roads to Yay-Hmyaun-Gyi Sakhan and also provide electricity supply to this area.' Another person commented.

Listening to their conversation, Khin Soe felt like reversing their modern concepts. 'If the Kyaiktiyo road is improved and modernized, won't it affect our livelihood?' Khin Soe felt anxious and concerned for the future.

* * *

'Hey Ma Kyi, I have brought the tomatoes you asked for. Here they are,' said Ma Shwe, as she entered and sat in a roadside hut. Ma Shwe would usually climb up the mountain to sell culinary goods. The woman in the hut who was breastfeeding a baby reached for the tomatoes and took them. She also bought other food items and vegetables.

Khin Soe's pilgrim group stopped beside the hut and tried to relax. The descent was faster. There was no need to rest often. The group was saying that they would spend the night at Yay-Hmyaung-Gyi. For Khin Soe, he could go straight down. But he would have to wait for his turn again so it would make no difference whether he got back to the base camp in a hurry, or not. The fees he received for one climb was sufficient for the family's food expenses for three or four days. Once this hike was completed, he could go to the labour office and try to stand in as a substitute carrier.

While Khin Soe was thinking, he noticed that Aye Mya and Aye Hla were not with them. Ngwe Moung and his sister had already gone down. So, even as the pilgrims went down, Khin Soe had to stay behind and wait for Aye Mya and her sister. They were taking a while to arrive and Khin Soe became anxious. They never walked at a slow pace, and while descending, their pace was in fact faster.

The ten-minute wait felt like forever. Just as he was contemplating whether to go up and look for them, Aye Mya arrived.

'What took you so long? And where is Aye Hla?'

'Her footwear snapped. And her feet are hurting.'

'No wonder. You should at least spend some money to buy a pair of firm and strong footwear. Well, you wait for her. Give me your basket. I'll go down first in case they need their clothes when they take a bath.'

Khin Soe took the basket from Aye Mya and lifted it onto his back. 'You take Aye Hla's basket and follow quickly, do you hear?'

'Alright, alright.'

Khin Soe adjusted the load and descended hastily. Even while he was descending, he was thinking, 'If the road they build leads to Yay-Hmyaung-Gyi, we shall have to carry the luggage only from that point. It will make it easier for us but it will reduce our carrier fees too.'

* * *

Even in the cool early morning, Khin Soe's forehead was sweating. Since Aye Hla's feet were hurting, he and Aye Mya carried one basket each. Khin Soe was thankful he had shared one basket with Ngwe Moung and his sister.

The pilgrims who were coming down the mountain looked radiant. They were beaming with pride because of their achievement. They even offered words of reassurance to those who had just started to climb up.

For Khin Soe, it was different. The closer he got to the base camp, the pleasure of completing the hike ebbed away and he felt more hesitant to get back to the reality of life. Was his father feeling better? His father, after being discharged from the hospital, had yellow eyes and suffered from fatigue and weariness. The last time Khin Soe received carrier fees was five days ago, so was there any money left to buy food today?

'Let us go down slowly, my grandson. We are almost there. Because you helped me, I could go up and down the mountain without having to rely on carriers. It is worth dying now that I have had the rare chance of worshipping this unique and unusual pagoda. And my grandson, because of the merit you have gained from helping me walk up to the pagoda, may you have health, wealth and become an educated person of high standing. Well done, well done, well done.'

Once Khin Soe got close to the grandson and grandmother pair, he heard the grandmother incessantly blessing her grandson. Khin Soe felt envious looking at the boy who was being repeatedly praised in abundance for helping his grandmother go up to the pagoda. 'My mother never once gave me blessings! Well, I have never helped her up the mountain to the pagoda. When father went up too, he never took mother with him saying she would be a nuisance. Next time, I will take mother up to the pagoda so that I may gain some merits,' Khin Soe thought to himself.

The rows of shops could be seen now. They were back at Kin Pun Sakhan. Khin Soe went straight to the labour office.

Soon after, Aye Mya and Aye Hla arrived. Once again, they had to weigh the luggage on the scale. Some luggage had been removed by the owners so it weighed less than before. Altogether they received a total of about 60 kyats, which meant 12 kyats for each carrier.

Khin Soe gripped tight the 37 kyats he had made and rushed home. Father was sitting on a bamboo bedstead in front giving finishing touches to the small sling fish basket he had made. Mother was at the back pouring out the surplus hot water from the rice pot. Little sister was sitting and playing near mother. Nobody greeted him with 'Are you back Khin Soe?'

'Mother, what curry do you have? I am famished!'

His mother pointed her chin at the pot of fish paste sauce. 'Wait a while. The rice is still very hot.'

Khin Soe sat on the floor. Then, from between his vest and his bosom, he took out the 37 kyats and handed it to his mother. He wondered to himself, for the first time, if his mother would bless him profusely like that old woman did.

His mother took his cash, put them into her pocket, and went out to the cleansing corner. The rice pot was emitting piping hot steam.

June 1980

Moe Kyaw, Resident of Kyaukpadaung, Mandalay Region

Moe Kyaw felt a deep-seated grievance against his father. But he could not air his grievance. Why? Because the grievance was against his own father.

There were seven offspring in their family. Moe Kyaw was the middle one with three elder siblings and three younger siblings. The two eldest sisters had already got married. One married a merchant from Taung-dwin-gyi. They were faring quite well. They could even support the family a little. The younger of the two elder sisters had recently eloped with an office clerk. Father was ashamed and enraged and threatened to give them a hiding. But father himself, when he was still a student with no job, had eloped with mother. But in their case, the parents-in-law were considerate and provided for them. Now, the sister could not make ends meet, let alone support the family so when father was around, she did not dare to come and visit them.

Moe Kyaw's immediate elder brother Soe Kyaw was father's favourite. Last year he passed the matriculation examination with two distinctions and then joined Meikhtila Regional College. The family had to send him 300 kyats every month but father never complained about it.

What father used to say was that of all his offspring, Moe Kyaw was the most thoughtless and tactless one, that he did not go to school regularly, that he was not industrious, that he was not purposeful, and that he was the most useless one, not holding a candle to his brother Soe Kyaw.

The two younger sisters were still students. Nilar Kyaw, who was only two years younger than Moe Kyaw, passed eighth standard that year. Moe Kyaw had to leave school before passing ninth standard. He had failed two times in a row. Even the youngest son Aung Kyaw was now in seventh standard. Moe Kyaw was the black sheep of the family.

But mother loved Moe Kyaw the best, even though father was not too happy about it. Why favour someone who was just a loiterer? He remarked that Moe Kyaw became a car driver because he didn't study, and that was not something admirable. And how much was he earning? He was the worst of the three sons. Even the younger daughter Nilar Kyaw was more competent. Those were the scathing words his father had for Moe Kyaw.

But who was the one beside father throughout his life? Somehow, father did not seem to realize or take note of this fact.

* * *

In Kyaukpadaung, mother's parents were quite well off. She was the only daughter so she had a carefree life. But true to the nature of a girl with a carefree attitude, she instinctively turned to romance. Therefore, in her adolescent years, she ran off with father who had no means of a livelihood. Father, while still in his youth, was trapped in the throes of married life. But he was an egoist and never admitted his mistakes. In fact, he could stand on his own feet only because the parents-in-law had supported them at the beginning.

Father drove long-distance buses between Kyaukpadaung and Nyaung-Oo. He saved every penny to buy a car of his own and prided himself for it. But he never mentioned that mother's parents looked after mother and the three children, so father had the opportunity to find ways and means to earn money without any worries for the family.

After Moe Kyaw's birth, father had his own car so the family started to live on their own. It was only then that his father started a life of his own. On their own with no one to support them, Moe Kyaw's parents were hard up. Never having considered previously the burden borne by the in-laws, father now became scared that he would not be able to make ends meet. The older the children grew, the louder their mother's complaints became and the father had to succumb to long hours of driving, which led to muscular stiffness and illness. When his two daughters married, it lessened his burden in a way. But father never considered things justifiably and was dissatisfied.

While two of his sons were doing well in school, father's health became poor and he could no longer lead an active life. His car also became inferior in quality like its owner. Father, mother, and Moe Kyaw realized that expenses, both for the car and for the family, were dwindling the family's saving. At the time, Moe Kyaw was enjoying life with his friends. When he came home from school and he slid under the car to help in his father make repairs, the older man did not appreciate it. Instead, he said, 'If you have an interest in cars, you will only become a car driver like me. It is not a worthy job.' This, despite the fact that in good times, father could finish up his work early and repose at leisure.

At times when father suffered from ill health and could not drive the car, he had to hire a substitute driver and send Moe Kyaw to go along as conductor since the young boy knew a fair deal about cars. But as usual, father did not appreciate it. He simply said, 'Now you get your heart's desire to become a car driver!' Moe Kyaw respond as he just wanted to alleviate his father's problems.

When too many days had to be spent as a conductor, Moe Kyaw missed classes and became an underachiever. It is not surprising that he failed the exam. While mother would count with trembling hands the money he handed to her, father would be praising his other son, Soe Kyaw, saying, 'He has cut his leisure hours and spends more time on studies. He will surely be an achiever!'

Later, father could no longer go along, even as a conductor. Because he had to rely on another driver, the income had lessened too. The situation called for Moe Kyaw to drive the car. He did not think twice. Just before his ninth standard exams were to start, he went down to Yangon and took driving lessons.

During Moe Kyaw's absence, father had to sell the car because the family needed money to send Soe Kyaw to university. In place of the old car, he bought an old Buick to run between Popa and Kyaukpadaung. When Moe Kyaw returned, father had become gaunt and skeletal yet the son had to dance to his father's tune. Along the bumpy road between Kyaukpadaung and Popa, Moe Kyaw had to drive his dilapidated little car with a full load of passengers three times a day. Though father could now stay at home in leisure, he did not see Moe Kyaw as his comrade. In his mind, the boy was just someone who drove the car because he did not want to study.

So how could Moe Kyaw help not nursing a sense of grievance against his father? But he could not air his grievance. Because the grievance was against his own father.

* * *

For today, this was the last trip. After the first two trips in the morning, Moe Kyaw thought of going home. Father had bought a car within his own means so the car was not too stout. But sometimes travellers who came from Bagan-Nyaung-Oo got to Kyaukpadaung quite late and wanted to reach Popa the same night. Mostly, they were happy to get whatever car they could, and Moe Kyaw would not let go of a chance to earn some money. So, he hardly took any rest. Gradually, his meal times and bed times slackened off but he did not care; if he could earn money, he would do it.

That day, it was a family riding in the car. When they started from Kyaukpadaung, it was past 6 p.m. and close to 7 p.m. He would have to drive quickly to get to the mountain base before dark. Before starting, Moe Kyaw dropped in at home; he had not eaten his dinner yet.

'Mother, what curry do you have?'

'There's some fish curry. If you like, I can make ponyaygyi salad for you.'

'Do not do it Mother. I am going for another trip. Pack my dinner. I'll eat it when I get to the mountain top.'

'It is too dark, Son. Will you pass the night up on the mountain?'

'Yes, Mother. I will have to make the descent only in the morning.'

Mother hurriedly prepared his dinner. Father was sitting on the bedstead in front chewing betel. Spitting out the spittle, he looked at Moe Kyaw and asked 'How much are you charging for a trip so late at night?'

'One hundred kyats to the mountain and back.'

'The car can hold twelve passengers. How many persons are there for this trip?'

'Only a family of five. How can there be a full load at this time?'

Moe Kyaw took the rice box and prepared to leave. He felt bad about making the passengers wait. They were in a territory unknown to them so they would be anxious to reach their destination before nightfall. Moe Kyaw had to reassure them that no harm would come to them.

'And you have to even pass the night there to wait for them!' Father, who was always an unfailing chider, said in a reproachful tone.

'But Father, of course I have to sleep there. How can I come down at such an hour?' Moe Kyaw retorted with impatience. His father, as he was out of work, drank a little in the evening, which made him rowdy and loud-mouthed.

'As if we do not know. Just because you want to sleep up there, you let go of earlier orders!' Father underrated Moe Kyaw that much. The boy stomped down the stairs and delivered a repartee to his father.

'Father, do not talk rubbish. I am doing my work the best I can. Please do not interfere.'

'Ah, how insolent! Son of a bitch! Just because you enjoy being a waif!'

Moe Kyaw suppressed his anger and walked briskly to the car. He was sure mother and father would be quarrelling once he left. Even when he occupied the driver's seat, his heart was still fluttering.

'Look boy, the sun is almost setting. You have no conductor and all. Are you sure you can do it?'

The woman in the car was asking him anxiously. Usually, Moe Kyaw brought a neighbour boy but on that day the boy was indisposed, so he did not bring him along.

'Do not worry Aunty. I usually frequent this road.'

'Alright then.'

Moe Kyaw's anger did not show in his voice but the hands that held the steering wheel still trembled.

* * *

Accustomed to driving three times a day on this road, Moe Kyaw's eyes and hands automatically controlled the car. Under the misty blue sky, the serene beauty of Popa brought nostalgia and tranquillity. The chill of the early winters could be felt. At this time of the day at the foot of the mountain, it was chilly all around. Moe Kyaw suddenly remembered Hla Lay Sein. A smile appeared on his face but all at once, remembering his father's spiteful words, the smile faded.

It was true that Moe Kyaw wanted to sleep on the mountain but he never slept there for the sole purpose of wanting to see Hla Lay Sein. He usually quit sleeping there as soon as he got passengers going down. And he never refused passengers solely because he wanted to sleep there. Though others might have said that his job was inferior but Moe Kyaw had a deep respect for his work. Even now he was earning from this job and that was how supported the family. He maintained his imperfect little car with the knowledge he had, and he treated the car with adoration.

They passed the vineyards. The view of Popa was becoming more distinct. A group of girls who collected firewood to sell waved from the roadside to stop his car. They usually hitchhiked in any car that passed by to get from one village to another. Moe Kyaw stopped his car. When they saw Moe Kyaw, they were delighted. No matter how much of a hurry he was in, Moe Kyaw always stopped his car for them.

'Hey, you must each give 1 kyat. No discount!' he teased them. 'We will, we will.'

The teenage girls shouted out with a high note and jumped onto the engine cover. They jostled against each other and balanced themselves so they wouldn't fall. The girls had to earn their livelihood the hard way. Moe Kyaw had respect for these girls who faced adverse circumstances just like him. How many aspiring and struggling youths like these were there around Myanmar? When Moe Kyaw went to Yangon to learn driving and car mechanics, he met many other boys who were in the same boat. They were the ones who were deprived of the pleasures of youth, in exchange for a source of income.

Adults like Moe Kyaw's father did not ponder over such conditions. Neither did they sympathize with the downtrodden.

The upcountry cold season suddenly whirled in, and it became chilly. The pretty girl in the car put on her sweater. The girls on the engine cover were enjoying themselves and singing happily as if they were on vacation. At one point, they got off and waved goodbye to Moe Kyaw. These girls who only earned a meagre sum of 1 kyat 50 pyas or 2 kyats energetically made their way into the forest and disappeared. Moe Kyaw's troubled mind began to dissolve, and he felt eager and enthusiastic. The bright lights from the circling level of the mountain were starting to be visible now. By this time, Hla Lay Sein would have closed her stall and would be helping out her uncle at his rice shop.

The small Popa village had begun to retire peacefully in the darkness of the night. On the way, some pilgrimage cars had stopped to rest. Moe Kyaw drove his car straight up to the circling level of the mountain. The night had become darker. The silence around them and the overwhelming darkness were alarming. The scent of the rich natural habitat engulfed them. The twists and turns of the road became plenty, and Moe Kyaw had to curb his wandering thoughts and drove the car more carefully.

'That was why I said it would be too dark,' the traveller aunty said in a frightened voice. 'Do not worry, Aunty. I am skilful in manoeuvring my car on this road at any time.'

It was easier said than done! At the hairpin bends, Moe Kyaw and other drivers had to drive cautiously all the while reciting prayers. If something went wrong, the car would fall down the ravine and cause undesirable loss. Moe Kyaw put his palms together and prayed to the mountain spirit. The traveller aunty did the same as Moe Kyaw.

When they finally reached the foot of the Taung-Kalat, the breeze from the surrounding environment made the atmosphere chilly. Moe Kyaw had to take the travellers to a monastery and requested the monk to place them in a zayat belonging to the monastery to rest for the night. After parking his car systematically, he proceeded to the rice shop where Hla Lay Sein would be. His passengers were also at the rice shop.

'Hey, young car driver, come and eat with us together.'

'It is okay, Aunty.' Moe Kyaw placed his rice box at the corner of the table. Hla Lay Sein could not yet be seen.

'You are young but you are such a skilful driver.' The tacit uncle praised Moe Kyaw.

'Yes really. The night was so dark and I was a bundle of nerves reciting a barrage of prayers. How many trips do you make each day?'

'Just two or three trips.'

'Oh, how well you earn a living at such a young age. You are such a good boy!'

It was for the first time that Moe Kyaw had heard praises from adults. The adult closest to him had never once praised him. That was why Moe Kyaw had a grievance against adults. He simply saw them as people who underestimated and suppressed the ability and power of struggling youths.

The guests ordered a variety of rice and curry dishes. Hla Lay Sein would be terribly busy. He had seen Hla Lay Sein only once that day.

'By the way boy, tomorrow when we go up the mountain, how about accompanying us?'

'Yes, I will, Aunty.'

Moe Kyaw glanced at the guest girl and nodded his head. The girl appeared to be the same age as Hla Lay Sein. But because she was dressed in nice clothes and had beautified herself, she looked more gorgeous than Hla Lay Sein. Even her soft yellow skin was totally different from the brown and rough skin of Hla Lay Sein. In fact, Hla Lay Sein was not pretty. But since she wanted to be pretty, she was called Hla Lay Sein instead of her real name, Hla Sein.

'Your sister cannot come out of the kitchen yet. This evening there are plenty of guests. Two busloads of pilgrims have arrived.' Hla Lay Sein's uncle called out to Moe Kyaw.

The girl guest glanced at Moe Kyaw. Without understanding why, Moe Kyaw was embarrassed.

The guests savoured the food with obvious relish. Despite of Moe Kyaw's refusal, they put chunks of curry into his rice plate. Only when the plates of the guests were being collected, Hla Lay Sein came out and collected them nonchalantly. Moe Kyaw realized at once that Hla Lay Sein was in a grouchy mood.

Without looking up at Moe Kyaw, Hla Lay Sein pulled away the plate in front of him.

Moe Kyaw pressed on the plate indiscernibly. 'Wait a little. I am not done yet.'

Hla Lay Sein took the other plates and turned away. 'Here, here, I have finished. You can collect it now.'

When she came out another time, Moe Kyaw called out to her. The guests had settled the bill and left already.

Hla Lay Sein came near him with a sullen look. Moe Kyaw took his rice box and put it on the plate. Usually, Moe Kyaw ate his rice box at the shop. The shop owner would give him some curry out of goodwill. After all, Moe Kyaw and the other drivers brought guests to the rice shops they had good relations with. Usually, Hla Lay Sein would clean and wash his rice box. But, today, she took the plate but put down the rice box on the table with a thump.

This morning Moe Kyaw had driven up two times but met Hla Lay Sein only once. Even then, they had no time to talk. They had just greeted each other. The travellers were ready to go down and Moe Kyaw hurriedly drank a cup of tea and dropped in at Hla Lay Sein's stall. At her stall, Hla Lay Sein sold beads, lacquer ware, ash trays, flower pots, hair clips, and hairpins. If there were many pilgrims, she would go up the Taung-Kalat to sell flowers. Hla Lay Sein was a hard-worker and she was as swift as the monkeys atop the mountain. One could not climb up and down the Taung-Kalat without getting tired. Even Moe Kyaw was tired after accompanying a group of pilgrims to the top. But Hla Lay Sein could do it easily three times in a row. Even that, she did not do it leisurely. She would walk close to the pilgrims and talk endlessly, saying things like, 'This is the cave where Mae Wunna gave birth.' 'This is the abode of Popa Medaw.' 'How about offering some flowers?' Most people, who were fatigued and impatient with her nagging voice, bought her flowers quickly.

When Moe Kyaw reached her stall that morning, Hla Lay Sein was busy selling her wares to customers, so they had not much time to talk. On the next trip, Moe Kyaw did not go to Shwe Gu corner but only to Popa town. So, she would have thought that Moe Kyaw went back without coming to see her.

Moe Kyaw washed his hands, took a cheroot, and went into the kitchen to light it. Hla Lay Sein was washing the plates. She did not turn to look at him. She always took advantage of Moe Kyaw. She had no parents and had to work for her living. Furthermore, she had to please the uncle who harboured her, so she helped him out at the rice shop. If the rice shop was crowded, she had to leave her own stall and come running to help at the rice shop. Otherwise, the uncle's wife would not be too pleased with her, in spite of the fact that they did not need to support her. The girl was grateful just for letting her stay with them under the same roof. This was another reason why Moe Kyaw felt that adults had no consideration or pity for youths. He respected and loved Hla Lay Sein as a comrade youth who had the courage to confront the vicissitudes of life.

'So many plates. Shall I help you wash them?' Moe Kyaw sat cross-legged on the floor beside Hla Lay Sein and said in a soft tone.

'Go away!' were Hla Lay Sein's first words.

'How can I go away? It's already dark. We are leaving only in the morning.' Moe Kyaw talked teasingly.

'Go away. You can sleep in your car.'

'It's too cold. I have no blanket. Shall I sleep near the kitchen?'

'If you are not scared of loud-mouth, you can sleep there!' Hla Lay Sein meant her aunt. But because Moe Kyaw always brought his passengers to their shop, the aunt was nice to him.

'Can you give me a blanket or something?'

'I will not. Cover yourself with your pasoe.'

'You are being cruel.'

'I have no pity for you. I cannot stand the sight of you.'

'Why may I ask?'

'Do not want to tell you.'

Hla Lay Sein put the washed plates on the rack neatly. Guests had begun to cease.

'I am tired. If you do not talk nicely to me, I am going to sleep. Have to get up early to take my guests up the mountain.'

'Hmm, I know.'

Moe Kyaw realized why Hla Lay Sein was peeved with him. 'What do you know, foolish girl?'

'Of course, I am a foolish girl. As for the girl passenger in your car, she is pretty like a porcelain doll and you could not even eat but gaze at her as if your eyes would fall out. This girl saw everything from the kitchen.'

'Stop it. Do not talk rubbish. I am unhappy because the old man at home said harsh words to me.'

Hla Lay Sein stopped her bandying words. She understood and sympathized with Moe Kyaw's life. She did not like Ko Mya Maung who wore a thick gold chain around his neck and spoke to her intimately. She preferred Moe Kyaw.

'Why quarrel with the old folk? It is good to have the chance to stay with your parents.' Hla Lay Sein said this as she longed to have parents around her. Her voice turned soft.

As usual, she looked at Moe Kyaw with piercing sharp round eyes.

'Yes, it is good. I did not say it was not good.' Moe Kyaw got up while puffing the cheroot.

'Are you coming with us to the mountaintop tomorrow?'

'Yes, I will follow from behind. Do not be gazing ardently at that young girl.'

'She is not as pretty as you. You have such big eyes and . dark complexion.'

'Stop it!' Hla Lay Sein did not like it if anyone said she had a dark complexion. Moe Kyaw patted her head and came out of the shop. Hla Lay Sein remained, pouting her lips.

Outside there was a strong wind. In the dark of night, the sound of the wind was becoming louder, making evident the influence of the surrounding deep forest land. The wind felt strong enough to blow one away. Moe Kyaw folded his hands tightly and walked to his car. He was tired and sleepy so he got into his car and prepared to sleep with his pasoe covering his body. The moment he closed his eyes, he heard someone knocking on the door. When he turned to look, it was Hla Lay Sein who opened the car door and threw in a blanket for him.

* * *

One had to climb with caution the narrow and steep steps. The strong wind was blowing with a roaring sound. Although they had intended to start early, they could not get up because of the cold. Some sunrays could be seen only after 7 a.m. If it stayed this way, it would not be possible to start back at 8 a.m., as they had intended toy. Moe Kyaw was sure to run into another problem with his father.

The monkeys were keeping close to them, shouting and jumping about asking for food. The higher one climbed, the objects below the mountain seemed tinier and tinier. Because of the dense mountain mist, the view afar was hazy and blurred. The objects on top of Taung-Kalat were only faintly visible in the misty fog. Nature was at its best bringing forth nostalgia, repentance, and religious thoughts. Moe Kyaw conjectured the love story between the Bagan hero Byatta and Mae Wunna of Popa, who was a happy country girl in the world of flowers. Due to her tragic love and attachment, Mae Wunna went through lamentations of grief and sorrow and died of a broken heart. Her beloved husband and her two young sons, the Shwe Hpyin brothers, all had lost their lives under the absolute monarchy system of those kings who wielded their power and autocratic authority.

He ascended slowly waiting for the guests. Before starting out this morning, he had returned the blanket to Hla Lay Sein and told her to follow them. She said she would. That day, after waking up, she had to help her aunt at the rice shop before opening her own stall. But Moe Kyaw did not have to wait long. While their group was resting at a stairway, Hla Lay Sein arrived with a bouquet of flowers that nobody knew when she had the time to pick. While the others had climbed the stairs leisurely, Hla Lay Sein had to climb in a hurry to catch up with them and was out of breath. But with thanakha applied unevenly on her cheeks, Hla Lay Sein's face looked bright, fresh, and energetic under the soft beams of the early morning sun. Moe Kyaw and Hla Lay Sein led the guests and climbed up leisurely. Along the way, Hla Lay Sein chatted familiarly with the monkeys. However hard she had to struggle for her livelihood, she was never slumped in dejection. Nor did she complain. She was not soft and delicate to look at but she had a lot of charm. The guest girl envied Hla Lay Sein's movements and climbed up briskly after them.

When they reached the top, the girl willingly bought flowers from Hla Lay Sein. And because Hla Lay Sein made quite a profit from selling the flowers, she even went and fetched water to change the water in the vase for the new flowers to be offered. The girl was no longer an object of jealousy to Hla Lay Sein.

When they started back, it was after 8 a.m. Moe Kyaw's mind was already on the motor road at the base. By this time, father would be waiting impatiently for him. He wanted Moe Kyaw to come back early from the mountain whether he got passengers or not. The car was beaten down and father did not like it to be kept idle. If Moe Kyaw did not arrive home in time, father would complain bitterly, 'This useless boy is deliberately wasting time!'

However, Moe Kyaw was considerate of others. He knew that pilgrims wanted to spend their time leisurely, looking around here and there. It would not be proper to hasten them. Since the travellers had given him ample fare for the trip, he did not want to annoy them. Hla Lay Sein realized Moe Kyaw's plight. While laying her stall, she had glanced at Moe Kyaw's disturbed face.

Ultimately, they started only around 10 a.m. Moe Kyaw's heart hung heavy. More haste, less speed! As soon as the car reached the plain ground, the engine broke down. Moe Kyaw had to wheedle and repair his little car, which had been coerced day in, day out. The repair took half an hour. The upcountry sun was heating up.

After he had sent the guests to their boarding place, it was almost noon. He would not be able to make two more trips that day. But if he was lucky, he could get passengers who would spend the night on the mountain although it was a period when pilgrims were becoming scarce.

The girl who did not speak a word on the way smiled and bid farewell to Moe Kyaw. Looking at the dainty and fragile face of the girl made him think of Hla Lay Sein with uneven thanakha patches on her youthful face. When the girl took the car fare from her mother and handed it to him, his fingers and her sharp fingernails touched.

The brand new 100-kyat notes were smeared all at once by the engine oil on Moe Kyaw's greasy hands.

* * *

That day, his father was surprisingly in high spirits. Moe Kyaw found out the reason soon. Father's elder son Soe Kyaw had come visiting. Moe Kyaw just took a glance at father and son talking together and went straight to the backyard through the kitchen. And despite his mother stopping him, he poured water on himself with a booming sound and washed himself.

'It is too hot son. You might get a heat stroke.'

'Do not worry, Mother. But why has your elder son come here? Is he here on vacation?'

'I do not know Son. What I overheard from their conversation is that he will be going to Yangon University.'

'Oh. What curry is there Mother? I am famished.'

'I have laid the table. It is pork curry.'

'Ah, what a nice dish. No wonder, the elder son is here!'

Moe Kyaw ate quietly. Usually, he liked pork curry but today it was not too delicious. He thought of the fish paste curry and vegetable side dishes from Hla Lay Sein's uncle's rice shop. No matter what, he decided to go and sleep tonight on the mountain.

'Hey Son, have you had enough? Why have you eaten only a small amount?'

Moe Kyaw took out his earnings of 100 kyats from his shirt pocket and handed the notes to his mother. He did not feel like speaking much.

'Here, take this.' Mother handed him some kyat notes as Moe Kyaw prepared to leave for the car terminal.

'Are you leaving again already? Why did you return so late today?' His father called out and asked him.

'The car's starter engine is not good.' Moe Kyaw replied curtly and came out of the room. Soe Kyaw got up and followed him.

'Are you leaving now? I will also come along.'

'I can leave only when I get passengers. Do not come along. It is too cold on the mountain.'

Moe Kyaw and his brother did not talk much even when they stayed together at home. Soe Kyaw went out to spend time with his friends. Moe Kyaw just loitered near his father's car. 'If you are interested in cars, you will just become a car driver!' The words father had spoken were quite true in a way.

Later, Moe Kyaw and his brother reached their car's parking place. Moe Kyaw got into the car and checked this and that. He slid under the car to check the starter engine. Then, he opened the bonnet and poked here and there. He refilled oil and water. Just like a jockey sprucing up his horse, Moe Kyaw spruced up his car. When satisfied, he puffed on his cheroot and sat down to chat with his driver colleagues.

Soe Kyaw could not stand the place. Without having to do anything, he was sweating all over. He was heated up. If one had to enter the car right now, how scorching hot it would be!

Some travellers going to Popa had arrived. They were divided equally into the two available cars. The car in the front left first.

Moe Kyaw threw away the cheroot and got into the car. He looked lithe and agile. Although the front door of the car was open, Soe Kyaw did not enter. Only the boy who usually accompanied Moe Kyaw entered and occupied the front seat. Realizing that Soe Kyaw was only trying to appease him due to a sense of guilt, Moe Kyaw smiled knowingly. He was satisfied so long as his hard work was acknowledged. Even if his brother was going abroad as a scholar, he would gladly let him go and support him the best he could.

'I am going now. Tell father I will be spending the night on the mountain.'

Moe Kyaw closed the car door. Soe Kyaw remained standing. He had looked wonderingly at this younger brother who worked ungrudgingly under the sun and who would be sleeping without much protection in the chilly mountain air.

Moe Kyaw started the car engine. The little car readily started. Moe Kyaw's feelings were not like the previous day. He was invigorated, and he started out on the trip radiantly and buoyantly.

At home, father would be praising and eulogizing the achievements of his beloved elder son, whom he considered a commendable youth of the future.

March 1981

Ma Tar, Resident of Magyeesin Village, Sagaing Region

'Ma Tar, wake up. You should not sleep so much. It is not becoming for a girl.'

'Ah, Mother, who told you girls are not entitled to sleep much?'

'You are always full of excuses. Look, Thin Mar and all have already left. The festival is just around the corner. You should try and sell as much as you can now.'

'I know. Just give me a few minutes.'

Ma Tar rubbed her eyes with the back of her hand and tried to wake up but she could not do it so she continued to lie down. She blamed the dawn for arriving so soon. She never had enough sleep. The earlier she needed to get up, the longer she wanted to sleep. Last night too, she had to help mother purify the beans so she could not go to bed early.

Mother got her boiled peas carrier bucket ready but not trusting her daughter, came into the room again and checked. When she saw that Ma Tar had drawn the blanket up over her head and was snoozing again, she whacked hard her daughter's hips two or three times. Ma Tar could not sleep on.

'Mother, I told you I was getting up!'

'Getting up, my foot! I have left a pot of plain green tea to boil on the fire. When your father wakes up, give him the leftover rice and some boiled peas I have left. Hurry up now. I am already late because I had to keep waking you up.'

Mother suddenly gave Ma Tar a kick and went out to the front of the house. Ma Tar could not be slothful so she rolled about and got up. She then went to the cleansing corner and scooped a cup of water with the coconut-shell cup. She heard her mother's voice from the top of the road shouting out 'boiled peas'. While washing her face, Ma Tar realized that her mother's voice when she was shouting out 'boiled peas' was not as loud and resounding as it had been last year.

Mother was a vigorous and energetic person. She was brisk and active and she could really work. Just as she could work, she wanted others to work like her. But mother was lenient with father. She felt bad that father had to work hard only after he married her. In mother's community, father was thought of as superior because he belonged to well-off parents.

Mother used to work at the flour mill owned by father's uncle. It was no wonder that father's relatives opposed the liaison between the boss' nephew and the flour mill labourer girl. But father married mother unequivocally and stayed true to her. This one thing was enough for mother to hold father in high regard.

Ma Tar washed her face and rubbed it dry with an old pasoe. Then she entered the kitchen. The pot with the plain green tea that mother had put on the fire was boiling and its steam was escaping with a loud hissing noise. Ma Tar removed some firewood from the fire. At about that time, her young brother Aung Htoo woke up and came into the kitchen.

'You will give me a bowl of rice, will you not?' Aung Htoo made this request before going to the cleansing corner.

'Hey, there is very little rice. I have to leave some for father too.' Ma Tar told her brother as she inside the rice pot. The rice was cold and hard to touch. But the plate of soft-boiled peas mother had left was still steaming hot. Ma Tar put the lump of leftover rice into a bowl and sprinkled the peas over it. Then she added oil and salt to the bowl and mixed everything lightly. By the time the plain green tea and rice were ready, father had woken up and come in. Out of the corner of her eye, Ma Tar looked at Aung Htoo who was standing beside her. She put some rice on his plate. She put father's share in a new plate and as for her, she just ate the remaining rice in the bowl. When father sat down at the low table to eat, Ma Tar and her brother had finished their breakfast of leftover rice.

'Hey, have you both finished? So quick.'

Ma Tar did not say anything but Aung Htoo could not contain himself. 'Of course, it was quick. There was little to eat!'

Ma Tar widened her eyes at Aung Htoo but the brother disregarded her. 'There is quite a lot on my plate. Here, take some.' Aung Htoo ate up what his father shared all the while saying 'Cannot believe mother sells boiled peas. Such a small amount of peas. Cannot even spot them!'

'Aung Htoo, eat quietly. Do not be talkative. Boiled peas are not meant to be eaten as a curry dish.' Ma Tar wanted to say more, 'Mother has to sell boiled peas and buy food for the day', but she didn't. Ma Tar was frank and outspoken just like her mother but at home, she practised a high level of tolerance for her father and brother. At the market, she was never humbled by anyone. On the platform of the Kaung-hmu-daw Pagoda, there was no one who dared to be in contention with Ma Tar.

Father did not eat up all that was put on his plate. It had been some time since father was not heartily eating his daily breakfast of leftover rice and a sprinkle—as Aung Htoo had complained—of boiled peas. Mother who left the house earliest did not know about it. Mother who loved father would be unhappy if she learnt of this.

Father handed his plate with the remaining breakfast to Aung Htoo and dressed up to go to work. He worked at a relative's blacksmith kiln. He could not be a supervisor like at the flour mill. He was just a worker. Mother did not want him to work in a lowly position but father was adamant. He had the hope that one day when the elders were appeased, he would be recalled to the flour mill. Ma Tar had turned sixteen already, but father was never contacted.

'I may be late today. Tell your mother.'

Father left. Aung Htoo finished up the leftover breakfast.

'Hey, can your stomach hold all that food? Such a lot you have eaten, just like an animated evil spirit!'

'If I do not eat like this, I get hungry at lunch hour. If you happen to have some cash, how about giving me some?'

'What? How can I have cash? Yesterday I had to give what I had to mother. I have been wanting to buy some clothes in time for the pagoda festival but I still cannot.'

'Just give me 1 kyat. Father told me he would give me some pocket money if he receives his wages this time. Then I will return your money.'

'I really do not have any.'

'Alright then.'

Aung Htoo grudgingly prepared to go to school. He was three years younger than Ma Tar and already in fifth standard. Ma Tar had to leave school before she passed fourth standard. Neither father nor mother was keen on the schooling of a daughter. Most of the other girls left school to become hawkers so it was not unusual for Ma Tar to become a hawker herself. She did not feel sad about leaving school. But mother used to tell Aung Htoo 'You must study hard. Only if you are educated, you will not be in a state of inferiority.'

So, Aung Htoo had to study.

There was no high school in Magyeesin so he had to go to a school in Sagaing. Father never complained about the expenses he had to bear for Aung Htoo. Aung Htoo was the most privileged person at home.

Ma Tar collected and washed the dirty plates. Afterwards, she sat before the mirror and beautified herself. Beautifying herself meant only putting on thanakha in uneven patches on the face. Even if one put on thick thanakha, one's complexion became dull under the upcountry sun.

Neither was it unusual to have one's face become oily after working under the heat. But this morning she dressed up in earnest. She evened out the thanakha with a toothbrush. Then, she put on her most modern jacket, the one with the puffed sleeves. After all, today she had a rendezvous with Win Hlaing. She took the popcorn bucket out of the house and closed the front door. There was need to lock it.

'The amount of popcorn is running out,' Ma Tar said to herself and went out to the main road. She waited for a horse cart heading to Kaung-hmu-daw Pagoda. Sometimes, instead of waiting, she walked to the pagoda but today she did not feel like it.

Ma Tar saw two horse carts, full of passengers, passing by.

'The number of pilgrims is increasing,' she said to herself again.

Kaung-hmu-daw Pagoda festival was just around the corner. It was a time when it was, indeed, profitable to peddle one's wares. Ma Tar and the other girls had to rely on such high days and holidays to earn more income.

'Hey Ma Tar, are you just going now? Come along with me.'

A horse cart stopped near Ma Tar. She saw Mya Shwe. Ma Tar turned her face the other way.

'You are acting as if seeing me is like seeing a ghost. I am inviting you with good intention.'

'No thanks. I would rather go on foot.'

'You never appreciate my good intention.'

Although Mya Shwe was just a horse cart driver, she was gushy with words. Unfortunately, her appearance was a disadvantage. She had a dark complexion and was buck-toothed. Ma Tar's friends took advantage of Mya Shwe's wackiness and rode her horse cart free of charge. Mya Shwe would smilingly take them.

As for Ma Tar, she could not stand the sight of Mya Shwe. Of all the girls, Mya Shwe favoured Ma Tar most. Everyone knew it and teased Ma Tar who hated it.

Now too Mya Shwe had stopped her horse cart and was waiting for Ma Tar. 'You go on your own, Mya Shwe.'

'I am going your way. You have a bucket to carry and all.'

It seemed as if Mya Shwe would not leave if she did not get on the cart. Ma Tar thought to herself that the earlier she got to the pagoda, the better it would be, so she hopped up onto the back of the cart. She placed her bucket on her head.

'Give me the bucket and move forward. I will not bite you.'
'Just drive. Do not ramble on.'

'Oh, you never have good words for me. I said it because the cart might be too heavy at the back.'

Ma Tar moved forward a little. The cart started out when Mya Shwe bawled out at the horse. Mya Shwe's face was animated. The horse cart was running at a fast pace. Big cars were driving by without decelerating so the cart had to be moved aside every now and then.

'The big cars have no mercy. If we do not move aside, they would just ram into us. Might is right; it is such a pity.'

'You talk big!'

'I say what is right.'

'Let it be, let it be.'

The sun was coming out. In the sunlight of the bright morning, the atmosphere of the pagoda and its surroundings was serene and restful. Under the soft and delicate sunlight, the summit of the pure white globular Kaung-hmu-daw Pagoda seemed to be reaching out towards the sky.

The Kaung-hmu-daw lake was also shining brilliantly matching and reflecting the sunlight.

'Just drop me at the top of the road.'

'Makes no difference. I will take you inside.'

She headed towards the façade of the pagoda. Not one pilgrim could be seen yet.

Thin Thin Mar and Khin Ohn Myint came running as soon as they saw Mya Shwe's horse cart.

'Hey Ma Tar, how very well you are doing! And Mya Shwe, hmm, you look pleased and delighted. Why you are smiling with a dreamy look in your eyes!'

When Khin Ohn Myint teased them, Mya Shwe was amused and laughed heartily baring her buck-tooth.

'Do not flatter a lunatic. I am sick of it,' Ma Tar said while throwing down her pair of clogs with a thud. Then, she hopped down lightly.

'You are too bad. You ride her cart and yet you have no sympathy.'

'Yes, tell her, tell her.' Mya Shwe handed down Ma Tar's bucket and said to the other girls.

'You girls, if you have sympathy, you are welcome to show her your sympathy!'

'Never mind if no one has sympathy. I have to go and pick up some flour bags at Tinn Tate.'

Mya Shwe reined in her horse to reverse and then clicked her tongue at the horse and started off on her way. Ma Tar knew Mya Shwe had gone out of her way to drop her, yet she refused to thank her. Although Ma Tar and Mya Shwe went to the same school in Tinn Tate when they were young, Ma Tar had no particular attachment for Mya Shwe. But Mya Shwe now bore a silly unabashed look and that made it worse.

Ma Tar carried the bucket on her hip and entered the pagoda square. The pure white Kaung-hmu-daw Pagoda stood gracefully under the shimmering sunlight.

'Today is a holiday so there will be many pilgrims. I have very little popcorn left. How about you? Have you bought some more?'

'Of course, we have. The price has gone up. It is 18 kyats now.'

Usually, one basket (of 16 pyi or bushel) of popcorn cost 15 kyats but now that the festival was drawing near, prices had gone up. But not to worry. They could sell more and make more profit. Another important thing for Ma Tar was to buy some material for a new jacket in time for the festival.

Some gooseberries had fallen on the pagoda square. The sun was not yet high so one could walk without scorching the soles. Some children were running around and playing.

When Ma Tar, Thin Thin Mar, and Khin Ohn Myint were spotted, Ah Win and a group of girls whispered to each other. Their group consisted of younger girls just over ten years of age. Ma Tar and her friends were maidens; at least, they considered themselves maidens. The difference was that they no longer ran around and played on the pagoda square. They walked daintily and dressed beautifully. But if a situation arose, they felt no restraint in pulling up the hem of their longyis and fight rowdily. But in vending their wares, age offered no advantage. Whether girl or maiden, one had to sell competitively.

The group of younger girls were quite scared of them. When they ran all over the place, selling their wares aggressively to the pilgrims, Ma Tar and friends had to scold them and keep them in check. Only then did the girls slow down.

From the pagoda square which had three enclosure walls, Ma Tar and her friends descended to the fish pond. The find vendors were already there. It was a bit early so the surface of the pond was still. Little fish and tortoises were lying low under the water waiting for food. Ma Tar and friends were also waiting for pilgrims to buy food from them.

* * *

Whenever a horse cart arrived, the girls all became active. Flower sellers shouted out shrilly to the pilgrims to buy their flowers. After paying homage to Kaung-hmu-daw Pagoda, the pilgrims would surely go down to the fish pond. For this reason, the young one were loitering around to show the pilgrims the way to the fish pond.

Ma Tar and the rest of the girls put their popcorn in small plates and waited for customers. The girls were not allowed to sell on the pagoda square. They had to queue up along the path from the pagoda to the pond. They prayed to the pagoda for customers who would buy a lot with benevolence.

But it was not quite to be.

Only four or five pilgrims came down. At first when they saw the girls queuing up, they did not seem to understand but when the girls all shouted in unison, they were alarmed and then they understood.

'Why, do you not buy some popcorn to feed the tortoises and fish in the pond? Please buy some portion from each of us.'

Ma Tar and friends were selling in a composed manner but Ah Win and group were forcing their plates into the hands of the pilgrims who could not help but buy from them. Otherwise, the girls were shouting at the top of their voices.

These girls were quite unmanageable. But sometimes Ma Tar and friends, although in despair, had to be considerate towards them. And so, the elder ones were left with unsold plates of popcorn.

Now too Ah Win was the most active, over-active in fact! She stuck close to a woman pilgrim and thrusted her plate of popcorn into her hands. The woman naturally had to buy it. But Ah Win did not stop there. Once she sold a plate, she ran to fetch another one from her friends and started the spiel again.

'Please buy from us also, Uncle.' That was all Ma Tar and friends could say. They were no longer young girls with locks of hair gathered atop and tied in a tuft, to run about like Ah Win and her group did. They had to keep their composure. Occasionally, they too tried to shove their plates into the pilgrims' hands, otherwise they would have sold nothing by sunset.

Ma Tar made 1 kyat from her first buyer.

Only when the pilgrims left did their shrill voices like minas on a red silk cotton tree quiet down all at once.

Three 1-kyat notes could be seen in Ah Win's hands. She looked so happy, that girl!

She asked her companion Aye Mya 'How much did you make?'

'I did not make any. I could sell only one plate. And they will give me the money only when they leave.'

'Well, I took one plate from you and sold it. Here is 1 kyat.'

What compassion they had for one another! Ma Tar took pity on them as they were so much younger. But they should be disciplined.

'Hey you girls. You should be careful with the way you sell. You are scurrying around and blocking the pilgrims. We have to sell too. It is not fair for you to grab all the customers.'

Ah Win did not take heed of others but she was somewhat scared of Ma Tar. 'But you got to sell too.'

'Look over there. Thin Thin could not sell any plate. You, you forced the same person to buy two plates.'

'It was her choice.'

'You were clinging to her. As if you were going to take off her longyi!' Ah Win pouted her lips and turned away.

'Do not say anything Ma Tar, they are so annoying.'

Thin Thin Mar was as soft as her name. In a way, she was submissive. That was why on days when the others earned 8 or 10 kyats, she could not make more than 5 or 6 kyats. But Thin Thin Mar's family was in more comfortable circumstances than Ma Tar's. Her parents were paddy growers.

Not long after, a big bus arrived. The girls knew that it was a pilgrimage bus from a distant place, and their faces lit up. Everyone became active. They put popcorn into plates and they waited. Ah Win who was shrewder than the others put less popcorn on her plates and ruffled them. Ma Tar turned to Ah Win and cast a side glance to caution her but Ah Win pretended not to see and turned her face the other way.

The fish in the pond knew nothing.

If they knew, they would be grateful to Ma Tar and the girls. These girls were waiting for people to feed them, were they not?

* * *

Every gazette holiday, it was customary that Win Hlaing came.

But he did not frequent the same place. His main place of work was at Sagaing Hill. But sometimes, he visited Mandalay Hill too. There were times when he stayed one whole week at the Maha Myatmuni Pagoda. If there were crowded pagoda festivals, he was there. He was a photographer by profession.

Win Hlaing was a Sagaing local. His appearance was impressive. He was lean, tall, and sported long hair. He looked good in pants. He was completely different from Mya Shwe.

Ma Tar got to know him last year before the pagoda festival, just like now. That day, while she was picking gooseberries under the hot sun, there was a sudden flash and she was alarmed. When she looked up and saw Win Hlaing standing upright with camera in hand, she was surprised at first but then she recollected herself and went up to him.

'Did you just shoot a photo of me?' Ma Tar was neither rude nor polite.

Win Hlaing slung his camera around his neck and looked at her smilingly, not irreverently, but Ma Tar felt insulted.

'I will not be able to pay for my photograph. You can make money if you take other people's photos instead of taking mine.'

Win Hlaing laughed with pleasure. He looked about five years older so perhaps he took Ma Tar as a child. Mother had remarked that Ma Tar had grown this year into a chubby and luxuriant girl. But because of her sloppy style and uneven thanakha patches, her appearance was not respectable at all.

'Who told you that you have to pay for the photograph?'

Ma Tar talked unfamiliarly but Win Hlaing talked to her as if she was a child. 'Then, why did you take my photo? And it would not be a pretty one either.'

He laughed again. She knew her photo had been taken while she was picking gooseberries in the sun.

'Do you want a nice picture? Then I will take some more.'

'Really?'

Did Win Hlaing take her for a laughing stock? The way she was wearing her mother's longyi with the upper hem cloth cut off looked disorderly and funny.

'Yes, I will.'

'I will not pay you, understood?'

'It is okay. No need to pay.'

'Then let us do it tomorrow.'

'What about now? The photo I took now is really good.'

'Oh, it cannot be. Why did you take it? Are you giving it to me?'

Win Hlaing looked again at Ma Tar as if she was a pitiful child. 'That one is for a photo contest.'

Ma Tar did not understand it well but she thought that if she asked more questions, she would sound silly. So, she stopped. She just felt happy for having helped him. Also, it was the first time she had made friends with someone of higher standing, so she felt proud.

The next day Ma Tar dressed with enthusiasm for the photoshoot. She announced to Thin Thin Mar and Khin Ohn Myint that she was going to have her photo taken by Win Hlaing free of charge. Her friends begged for a chance to have their photos taken too.

They all dressed up smartly and waited for Win Hlaing. He arrived only at noon when the sun was scorching. Looking at their faces with sweat lines running down their thanakha patches, he gave a laugh.

'Look here. My friends also want to have their photos taken. They are paying but of course at a discounted rate.'

Just then, some pilgrims arrived and Ma Tar and her friends had to run and peddle. After that, they waited a while as Win

Hlaing took photos of a group of pilgrim girls. By that time, their clothes and make-up were already quite dishevelled.

But, even so, the photos taken by Win Hlaing were memorable and the girls all became friendly with Win Hlaing. If he was dozing under the sun with a signboard full of photos beside him, Ma Tar and all would tease him and clown around just to amuse him. Sometimes, they pelted him with gooseberries and ran away. Some the children stuck moustaches on the photos of actresses on the signboard since nobody knew who the photographer really was. Win Hlaing would get angry but he could not blame them. After all, it was these children who enticed pilgrims saying, 'Hey sister, why do you not have some pictures taken as keepsake?' and then brought to him the customers.

Sometimes when Win Hlaing got plenty of customers there or he had earned plenty from another place, he would buy plates and plates of popcorn from the girls to feed the fish. Then, Ma Tar and all who had never fed the fish for nothing would all join in and feed them with the popcorn Win Hlaing had paid for.

This year they did not hang out with Win Hlaing as much as before. Ma Tar, Thin Thin Mar, and Khin Ohn Myint had all developed into big and tall girls; their childish behaviour was fading away. They no longer pelted Win Hlaing with gooseberries but looked at him shyly. They wore their longyis with slink and they walked with poise so Win Hlaing would no long treated them as children.

Ma Tar thought more highly of Win Hlaing than Mya Shwe because Win Hlaing was stylish and composed whereas Mya Shwe was a barefaced tease. Ma Tar began to look forward to seeing Win Hlaing who came to the pagoda once or twice a week. But the feeling was not unusual. She relied on Win Hlaing as a brother and was fond of him, that was all. But she was quite scared of Thin Thin Mar and Khin Ohn Myint who were chatterboxes. In front of them, she dared not show her interest in Win Hlaing. Did that mean she felt something for him? She was not sure. But her feelings, which were flitting about like a leaf, were not composed at all.

One day, Ma Tar was waiting for Win Hlaing eagerly.

She specially missed Win Hlaing on days when the pagoda was crowded with pilgrims. She felt contented to see him snapping photos. But, today he was late.

Pilgrims trickled in but he was nowhere to be seen. Even Ma Tar and friends had sold their plates of popcorn among a scrum of sellers and earned about 5 kyats each. The sun was coming up in degrees. The pagoda platform was hot from the sun and one could feel the intensity of the heat when walking barefoot. When there were no visitors, the girls took shelter under a gold mohur tree. Those who had brought rice packets, untied the packets and ate. Ma Tar considered the leftover rice and boiled peas she had eaten in the morning as her lunch. She could buy something to eat but she did not want to spend the money she had earned.

Ma Tar sat under the gold mohur tree which was drooping under the sunlight. In the early spring, the trees sported a flamboyant display of bright red flowers that bloomed profusely. The girls would gather around and spend their time under the tree amidst the fallen flowers. The yellow marigold flowers of the season were also wilting under the heat of the sun.

When Ma Tar was getting a little drowsy, Win Hlaing arrived. When she opened her eyes, she spotted Win Hlaing. As usual, he had his camera around his neck.

'Hey, why are you dozing off here all alone? Where are your companions?' Win Hlaing asked taking off his cap and sitting down. He was sweating. He had long hair so it was hot to look at him. He put his camera beside him dejectedly.

'Thin Thin Mar and all are having lunch. Brother, why are you late today? There were quite a lot of visitors this morning.' Ma Tar and the other girls all called Win Hlaing 'brother'.

'I was on the hill. Whoo, the sun is so very hot!' Win Hlaing was fanning his chest with his cap.

'Brother, you are an upcountry native. Why are you so afraid of the heat? The hot season is not yet in.'

'Upcountry natives can feel the heat too. It cannot be helped. Although the hot season is not yet in. Have you never heard that Tawthalin[1] sun can kill prawns?'

Win Hlaing and Ma Tar were used to talking familiarly. Win Hlaing took out a film roll from the camera and put in a new one. He tried the shutter. Under the sunlight, Kaung-hmu-daw Pagoda was standing majestically on its own. The stone lamp posts were standing erect.

'Brother, will you be opening your shop during the festival days?'

'Of course, I will. The festival days are what I have been waiting for.'

'You earn a lot of money, Brother.'

Win Hlaing reached out and patted Ma Tar's head. 'No, not really. I have a mother and a younger sister just like you.'

'Oh, you have a younger sister, have you? You never told us. Is she pretty?' Win Hlaing laughed. He had the habit of laughing with delight at conversations. 'Of course, she is pretty. Not dark like you but very fair.'

Ma Tar pouted her lips. 'Why, did you not bring your little sister?'

'How can I? She has to go to school.'

'Oh, she goes to school, does she?'

---

[1] September.

Ma Tar became reflective. Since she left school, she had forgotten about school and she had no interest in school lessons. To her, those lessons belonged to a different world. Now she was hearing that Win Hlaing's young sister was a schoolgirl.

'Brother, what standard is your young sister in?'

'Eighth standard.'

'How clever! How about you, Brother? You do not go to school?'

'I did. I passed ninth standard. But I left because I have to earn money.'

Ma Tar looked with respect at Win Hlaing who was working to support his mother and sister. She pondered how nice it would be if she had an elder brother like him.

While they were talking, Thin Thin Mar and the others came running.

'Brother, why did you not come? Please take some photos of us,' they shouted in unison. They handled Win Hlaing's camera one after another. Since everyone had made good money today, they were all in a good mood.

Right then, they saw a small car entering the precinct. The brand of the car could not be identified. A group of swanky guests including two or three girls got out of the car, so Win Hlaing stood up and prepared his camera. Ma Tar and all turned and ran to the pond to sell popcorn.

Of the group, only about three adults came down to the fish pond. The girls did not come so Ma Tar was glad thinking Win Hlaing was occupied in photographing them. Because she was thinking about him, she was slow to scamper and sell popcorn. And as expected, Ah Win scurried and blocked the pilgrims so Ma Tar and the others lost their chance. This time, Ma Tar could not be bothered to bandy words with Ah Win but ran back up to the pagoda square.

As she had thought, Win Hlaing was holding his camera in style and shooting.

The girls being photographed were youthful and pretty. Not like upcountry girls. Their way of dressing was stylish and modernized. Win Hlaing did not see Ma Tar. Even if he saw her, he would not be able to greet her. He was trying to please the girls by showing them a variety of suitable poses. He had to entice them to take more photos. Only when the elders completed their round of the pagoda, the girls stopped their photo session.

Ma Tar felt impatient looking at the girls and Win Hlaing treating each other with familiarity. So, she stopped looking and went to sit under the gold mohur tree. There, she was not even capable of concentrating to sell popcorn. And even though she was not exactly looking, she could see them out of the corner of her eye. The girls were writing something for Win Hlaing. Ma Tar could guess they were writing down the address where the photos were to be sent.

Ma Tar was not someone to envy other people's blissful lives but today, for the first time, she felt dissatisfied with her life. Win Hlaing's younger sister was going to school and already in eighth standard. As for her, she could barely just read. So, she knew nothing besides helping mother handpick peas, cooking rice, and selling popcorn. She did not feel lacking in anything. Her brother, Aung Htoo, going to school had nothing to do with her. But the thought that girls also had the right to education came to her mind today. Would she have to sell popcorn her whole life?

'Hey, what are you sitting here for? Are you not selling popcorn?' Win Hlaing saw her and asked. Ma Tar kept silent. 'Hey, did you not hear my question? I had a good day today. I made a lot of money so I am going home now.'

Win Hlaing never stayed long at the pagoda. His main shop was on Sagaing Hill. This place was not quite remunerative except during festival days. He was gathering his camera and film rolls. Ma Tar was sitting and moping, gazing at the yellow marigold flowers.

'Brother Win Hlaing. You made a lot of money, did you not ? Come and buy popcorn to feed the fishes. You will gain merit,' Khin Ohn Myint and Thin Thin Mar, who usually took advantage of their friendship with Win Hlaing, came to invite him.

'Go away. You make good money too. I earn a little better only during these days. Here is a girl who is moping because she could not sell much. Call her and take her with you. Do not be selling all by yourselves.'

'Ah, we cannot sell by ourselves either. Those other girls are vying with us. We cannot admonish them. Are you already going back Brother? More people might come in a while.'

Ma Tar did not join in.

'Yes. I am going back. I will return on festival days,' saying this Win Hlaing slung his camera and started to leave. 'Hey girl, why are you moping? Go and sell. I will shoot pretty photos of you on festival days. Win Hlaing patted Ma Tar's head and left.

'Come on. Why are you sitting here? Are you pettish with brother Win Hlaing? He has already left. With Mya Shwe, you have a raw deal. But with Ko Win Hlaing you have nothing.'

'You girls, do not say bad things about me.'

Ma Tar went along with them and after crossing three walls, they came to the pond.

Ah Win and other girls were happily horsing around. Never once could you hear from them that they wanted to go to school.

* * *

'Well, if you do not want to sell popcorn, what else do you want to do?' Mother puffed on her corn leaf cheroot and asked.

Father was sitting on the front floor chewing a betel quid leisurely. Aung Htoo was face down on the floor learning his lessons.

'Yes really. She is no longer young.' Father spat the betel spittoon down the floor gap and wiped his face clean of betel leaf bits.

'How can we let her do nothing?' Mother said while wetting her finger with saliva and touching the cheroot sparks.

'Just the other day I met Thein Saung,' father said after thinking for a while.

Thein Saung was the son of father's uncle. He was younger than father. Being a proud man, father did not contact any of his relatives but Thein Saung was fond of father and came visiting every once in a while. And whenever he came, he gave some pocket money to Ma Tar and her brother. He had offered to bear the schooling expenses for Aung Htoo too but father did not accept it. Father was embittered because his uncle had himself cut off relations with him.

'Thein Saung has not come for quite some time. What did he say?'

'That Uncle is not well. He appeared to have asked about me and the children.'

On hearing father's words, mother's face lit up. 'Now, at the flour mill, I guess Thein Saung is the only one working?' Mother asked with expectation. Uncle had only one son.

'Yes, but he has gained a lot of skill in his work.'

Mother's face returned to normal. Then, just to show that she was minding her own business, she continued puffing on her cheroot.

'Thein Saung must have told his father about the children. So, I guess Uncle said that . . . '

This time Ma Tar was all ears. She looked at her father with expectation. Mother also put down her cheroot to listen. Aung Htoo stretched his back from being absorbed in studying his lessons and glanced at his father.

'What was it that Uncle said?' Mother asked, looking impatiently at father who was chewing betel.

'What Uncle said was, if the elder daughter is no longer going to school, why do not we send her to their place since Aunty Mya is in need of a reliable companion.'

Mother was visibly happy although Ma Tar was not. But she summoned up the courage to say a few things to her parents. It was opportune as father was in a tolerant mood today.

'I can go and stay with Aunty Mya. But can you tell her to send me to school?'

Her sudden words made father's face shrivel and mother looked at her with surprise. 'Dear me! What ideas have you hatched up?' Mother said as if Ma Tar had said something unthinkable.

'Mother, what is wrong with saying I want to go to school?' Ma Tar and her mother were used to arguing heatedly. Ma Tar would say what she thought and her mother with her simple thoughts would argue back.

'She must have said it because, perhaps, she really wants to go to school.' Father said with sympathy for her daughter.

Mother could not understand it at all and was shaking her head repeatedly. 'What rubbish! When food and shelter is crucial and someone is asking for you, you should be humble. If you are tactful, you will be rewarded. Do not go and say you want to go to school and all that. You said you no longer want to sell popcorn. How convenient this is!'

Father did not put in a word. Ma Tar realized that father letting her go to his uncle's house was his utmost compliance. Mother was glad believing it was the start of a positive opening. But she was not too happy about Ma Tar's irrelevant request.

For Ma Tar, this seemingly foolish once-in-a-lifetime whim would remain unfulfilled, and this her sad. But Aung Htoo who could not contain himself interrupted and said something, which made her whim billow out once and for all.

'Elder sister, you say you want to go to school but from which standard would you start? You are too old to go back to fourth standard and it would be embarrassing!'

'Yes, really.' Mother joined in.

Ma Tar blamed no one but herself. Father ignored all of them and went out of the room.

Mother headed to the kitchen to prepare for tomorrow. Aung Htoo continued studying. Ma Tar remained, repentant and regretful for having attempted something she should not have.

* * *

The festival was around the corner so the construction of stalls and pya zat tents had been completed. Some sellers had already come and settled at the stalls with their pots and pans. Upcountry pagoda festivals were enjoyable, and the simple and honest upcountry natives enjoyed themselves at times like this.

Both children and adults were happy thinking that they would have the chance to watch Anyeint pwes and marionette puppetry shows the whole night through. After the Thadingyut festival would come the Tazaundaing festival, where Sein Aung Min's dance troupe will be performing. All the farmers who had been working tirelessly in the rice fields would enjoy themselves immensely. Upcountry maidens would spend their savings on beautifying themselves, wearing their best attire that would go with their brown skin. Nothing else was needed.

But this sudden whim that had come to Ma Tar's mind soon went away. It was festival time, and each of the girls would be making 8 to 10 kyats daily, so they all were eagerly waiting. At such times, there was nobody who was dissatisfied with his or her life. Ah Win and the group of young girls were noisily playing and selling to the many pilgrims who came visiting.

To upcountry natives, those who came from lower urbanized areas, this was a novel sight. Young or old, these visitors wore innovative items of clothing. Women as old as Ma Tar's mother went about wearing brightly coloured clothes. Ma Tar remembered her mother who did not have even one new longyi made for herself in a year. So, Ma Tar thought of going to stay at Aunty Mya's place, and if she got some money, she would give it to her mother.

One after another group of pilgrims arrived and Ma Tar and the rest were tired running to and fro selling popcorn.

Since selling on the pagoda platform or at the pond was prohibited, so it was a difficult task convincing the visitors into buying popcorn.

'Aunty, please buy some popcorn. There are plenty of fish and tortoises in the pond. Please buy, Aunty. The way the fish nibble the popcorn is a beautiful sight.' Ma Tar and all talked indiscriminately until the guests became somewhat interested.

'Ok then, give me a plate. How much is it?'

'Only 1 kyat per plate, Aunty.'

'Oh, so expensive.'

Trying to get money from rich people was not an easy task. The woman took the popcorn plate Ma Tar was shoving towards her and checked the contents.

'Such a small amount of popcorn. Make it 50 pyas.'

'Please do not bargain, Aunty. The buying price is high.'

'Hey, popcorn is cheap and plentiful.' The woman had taken the plate but was bargaining so Ma Tar was in a fix.

'The price is fixed, Aunty.' Saying so, Ma Tar followed close to the woman.

Ah Win and group were sharp and shrewd. They were not restrained by fear the of offending anyone.

Ah Win approached one man who was undecided whether or not to buy.

'Uncle, there are plenty of fish and tortoises in the pond. Please buy popcorn to feed them.'

'Really?'

'Yes, Uncle. Such a lot of tortoises.'

The man took two plates. But the tortoises and fish had so many people feeding them that they no were no longer enthusiastic to come up to the surface. It was an amusing situation. The man who fed the fish seemed to be a jolly person. But, in a few minutes, he came back from the pond. He was fat and was wearing a Hawaiian shirt that made him look funny.

'Hey, I did not see any fish and tortoises in the pond. You tricked me into buying the popcorn!'

'We did not trick you, Uncle. There really are plenty of tortoises.'

'I did not see any. Give me back my money.'

'No, I will not.'

'Then I will not return your plates.'

Ah Win knew the man was teasing her but he really took the plates with him so she had to run after him. The man put the plates into his leather bag and left.

'Please give me back my plates.' 'I will not. You tricked me.'

He went in the direction of the pagoda wall so Ah Win was frantic. She had no more plates left to sell to the next guests.

Ah Win's juvenile face was close to tears. The man got into a car. Ah Win ran after it. 'Give me back my plates. Please give me back my plates.'

There was a babble of laughter in the car, then her plates were returned to her. 'Such a tricky girl.' Ah Win heard the man mumbling a remark. She paid heed to no one and ran back to her place.

'Sister, why do you not buy some popcorn. There are plenty of fish and tortoises in the pond.' Ah Win's shrill voice erupted again with her genuine casualness. After all, what was more important to Ah Win than to sell plenty of popcorn?

In the pond, the fish and tortoises who had eaten their full were swimming placidly.

* * *

'One fish, two fish, three fish.'

So counting, the fish were let free into the water. 'May I be freed ten times for freeing you one time.' Thin Thin Mar wished.

At first, the little fish stayed still. But after a moment, they swam to the side at ease. Did they realize they had been set free?

Ma Tar gave 3 kyats to Daw Nge who sold live fish. 'Girl, you are freeing fish and all. Well done.'

'She is now well-off so she can afford to free fish.' 'Oh, really?'

'Yes. In future, you will no longer see her selling popcorn here.'

'Glad for her. As for me, it seems I will have to keep selling fish my whole life. I have to console myself by thinking of it as charitable work.'

Daw Nge took every word Thin Thin Mar said to be true, who bought live fish from the fisheries and sold those at the pagoda to be freed in the pond. The pond was a sanctuary.

'Daw Nge, she was just joking. Just think. How can I become rich all of a sudden?'

'But she just said you will not be selling popcorn anymore.'

'Yes, that is true. I am going to stay at grand aunty Mya's place.'

Daw Nge knew grand aunty Mya well. And everyone at Tinn Tate village knew Daw Nge to be a brilliant person.

'Hey, your grand aunty Mya is a rich lady. Your father is her nephew, is he not ?'

'He is related from grand uncle's side.'

'Whatever, it is no joke that they are calling you to stay with them. Selling popcorn here your whole life will not get you anywhere. Behave well. It will be to your benefit.'

Daw Nge had the same advice as Ma Tar's mother.

But Ma Tar could not yet discern if her life was really going to improve. All her life she had been nifty running around and playing and working as a seller. She began to feel nostalgia for the pagoda square. Out of all the money she had earned with blessings from the pagoda, she could only now spend 3 kyats to free some fish.

But for Ma Tar, it was a big donation.

On this day, Thin Thin Mar also was not selling popcorn. She was going along with Ma Tar to Tinn Tate village. Thin Thin Mar's family had told her that she was no longer needed to sell popcorn; instead, she could help out in the rice fields. Perhaps, the girls were now fully grown adults.

The shrill voices of Ah Win and other girls made them realize that new pilgrims were arriving. Daw Nge took her place and prepared to sell live fish.

'Free some fish in the sanctuary pond. Make a good deed while you are here.' Daw Nge shouted in a soft tone.

'How much is the live fish?'

'Five for 1 kyat.' Thin Thin Mar could not stay silent when there were buyers.

'Were these fish caught from this pond?' One woman enquired.

'No one is allowed to catch fish from this pond. Females are not even allowed to touch the water with their feet.' Ma Tar joined in and explained.

Only then did the woman buy the fish with a definite conviction. She took out 2 kyats from her big leather bag and bought ten fish.

'Give me two extra. You will gain merit' The woman persisted to give her extra fish. It was not known if the merit would go to that woman or to Daw Nge!

At times, it was interesting to watch pilgrims from various places. Sometimes, tourists would arrive and look in amazement at Kaung-hmu-daw Pagoda and make comments. The elder would say that the pagoda was built during the reign of King Thalun. How many workers must have been employed to build so big a pagoda? The brickyard where the bricks for the pagoda were baked had now been turned into a prominent fishery.

Win Hlaing arrived just before Ma Tar and Thin Thin Mar were about to leave. Ma Tar had come to the pagoda that day to bid farewell to her friends but she wanted to see Win Hlaing too.

'Brother Win Hlaing, Ma Tar has come today to bid us farewell. She will not be selling here anymore.'

'Really? Then we will be saved from her rasping!' Win Hlaing was trying to be comical but Ma Tar felt sad.

'Do not be sad. I was only joking. I myself will not be coming here in the future. I am going to Bagan with good company. I might get some business on the side.' Win Hlaing said as he looked at a pouting Ma Tar and appeased her.

'Brother, your work is so accommodating. Wherever you go, you can earn money.' Thin Thin Mar commented and, as usual, Win Hlaing laughed.

'You do not understand a thing. Do you know how hard it is to earn money? Come rain, come shine, you have to go around. You also have to entice people to hire you. And there are costs for film rolls, photograph paper, and camera repair charges. Not much profit left. Sometimes, if the photos sent to the addresses they had left are returned unclaimed, so much the worse.'

Thin Thin Mar laughed with pleasure. 'Then do not work as a photographer anymore, Brother.'

'I do what I know best. What else should I do?'

'Nothing!'

'How will I earn money if I do nothing? One has to be doing something.' Why do you not become an actor, Brother?'

'This girl!'

Win Hlaing patted Thin Thin Mar's head because he knew she was joking around.

That day, Ma Tar and Thin Thin Mar sat under the plum tree and waited for Win Hlaing who was taking photographs. He did not have a lot of customers that day. The festival was over so pilgrims were getting few and far between.

Afterwards, they paid homage to the Kaung-hmu-daw Pagoda and the three of them left together. Under the faint sunlight of the evening, the pagoda remained calm, peaceful, and majestic.

* * *

'Behave well at other people's place. Work to their satisfaction. And do not talk heatedly like at home. Act befittingly.' Mother was telling Ma Tar over and over.

Ma Tar was the key in the relationship between father's uncle—who was like a father to him—and father's family. That was why her mother was teaching Ma Tar all the essentials. Ma Tar kept nodding her head to please her mother. If she argued with her mother, as was her habit, the coaching would be never-ending.

Ma Tar arrived at her granduncle's place with what little clothes she had.

'Just look. How grown up she is! And she is a pretty one like her mother. But do not be foolish like your mother. If you stay with us, you must behave with decorum and not be negligent.'

The half-praise half-blame words she heard on arrival made her feel constrained. But a good future for her existed in that place so based on that perception, she decided to follow her mother's words.

Soon after, she had to listen to Grand aunty Mya's hard and fast rules.

'A girl must get up early. Prepare a pot of boiled water. And housekeeping must be done to keep the house neat and tidy.'

In the village, grand aunty's house was the tallest and largest. The family managed more than one business and they were well-organized. Whatever they earned was systematically saved.

Ma Tar had to get up early in the morning, clean the house, and prepare breakfast. Grand aunty Mya did not even buy breakfast snacks. Sticky rice had to be steamed at home. Grounded sesamum, coconut shreds, everything had to be prepared at home. The curry dishes constituted of tamarind leaves and acacia leaves from the yard, but there was ample food for everyone.

'Hey, if you are free, polish the floor. A girl is graceful only if she is working.'

Grand aunty Mya kept an eye on Ma Tar all the time and made her work ceaselessly. In the end if there was nothing else to be done, she was sent to the flour mill to help the female labourer there. Ma Tar was amazed at her mother's ability to snatch father out of the clutches of such a thorough and meticulous aunt!

At Kaung-hmu-daw Pagoda square, Ma Tar had to run, shout, and sell popcorn but she had a free happy life. Here, Ma Tar was kept busy all the time and scolded too.

'Hey, come here. If you have finished putting away the pots and pans in the kitchen, come walk on my body to relieve the stiffening muscles.'

When Ma Tar used to sell popcorn, she could lay down on the bed in a state of exhaustion as soon as she got home. Now, she could not go to bed without grand aunty's permission. She led a sheltered life but was miserable.

It wasn't even one month when Ma Tar went back home to her mother.

'Mother, I do not want to stay at their place. The whole day I have to be at their beck and call. I am not even allowed a moment of freedom.'

Mother pressed her chest with her hand. 'Hey, you are leading an anxiety-free life and still you are complaining. Look at you now. You have put on weight and your complexion is fairer. Does doing chores inside the house make you tired?'

'I do not like housework. I want to do another kind of work.'

'But you, yourself said you no longer wanted to sell popcorn. What else do you want to do?'

'Any work, but not at the beck and call of other persons.'

'They are not other persons. They are your relatives.'

'Relatives who do not seem likely to remunerate me for my services.'

'You are fed and clothed. What else do you need?'

'No, I want to work on my own and eat with what I earn.'

In her mind, she heard Win Hlaing saying, 'Everyone should be doing some kind of Work,' but she did not know how to say it to mother.

'You do not want to work under the sun and you do not want to work in shelter. Do not talk high and mighty! Just go back and stay there with quietude.'

At mother's command, Ma Tar had to go back to Grand aunty Mya's place.

* * *

One year and one month passed by but mother's expectations were not realized.

It was true Ma Tar was fed and clothed well but not a pya was given to her for her services. To say the least, even Ma Tar's clothes were bought and made by grand aunty alone. Ma Tar was not allowed to handle any money.

When Ma Tar used to sell popcorn, she could give mother what she had earned after keeping aside some for her clothes. She could also give some pocket money to her younger brother, Aung Htoo. The money father earned was not much and spent on Aung Htoo's school expenses and food for the family. The money mother earned from selling boiled peas was a supplement for miscellaneous household needs. Now, besides the fact that Ma Tar was absent from home, nothing had changed.

Ma Tar's pleas to let her return fell on deaf ears. Mother still had not lost her simple hope that one day, Ma Tar would get a chance at her grandaunt's place. But Ma Tar knew the real situation. Grand aunty Mya and family took Ma Tar in only as a trusted companion and nothing more. No chances were given and never would be.

Staying at grandaunt's place gave Ma Tar's complexion a healthy glow and she looked beautiful, but she had lost the happiness and freedom she had at Kaung-hmu-daw Pagoda square. She had no friends or companions. The only one she saw quite frequently was buck-toothed Mya Shwe who lived in the village. Whenever she passed the house with her horse cart, she would shout out greetings wearing a big smile. Although grand aunty did not like Ma Tar to talk with other boys, Mya Shwe was forgiven perhaps because Ma Tar herself favoured Mya Shwe or because grand aunty herself sometimes asked Mya Shwe to run errands for her.

Sometimes, even Ma Tar had to take Mya Shwe as a companion. 'Mya Shwe, if you pass by our place, please ask if my mother's health is alright. And tell Aung Htoo to come visit me.'

'Yes. I will. For you I would do anything.'

'Do you see Thin Thin Mar?'

'No, I do not. She also no longer sells at the pagoda.'

Mya Shwe was pleased because Ma Tar was treating her with special attention. 'How about brother Win Hlaing?'

'Which brother Win Hlaing?'

'The photographer Win Hlaing. He used to ride your horse cart.'

Of course, Mya Shwe knew Win Hlaing. Her face fell all at once. 'How would I know? I am not watching out for him.'

At times like this, Mya Shwe would jounce onto her cart laden with flour bags and leave immediately.

Ma Tar laughed with amusement. She was homesick for the home which was so close yet so far. And her friends. She also missed the worn-out 1-kyat notes she earned after quarrelling with Ah Win and the girls.

* * *

'I heard that Ma Tar's mother's health is under the weather.'

Ma Tar who was massaging grand aunty's neck stopped moving her hands. 'Uncle U Thein Saung, what is wrong with my mother?'

'Oh, a bit unwell here and there, perhaps.' Grand aunty shook it off as an unimportant matter. She herself was over fifty but still going strong. But her life had no struggles unlike mother.

'I did not get to the house. I only heard what others said.' 'Grandaunt, I am going to my house.' Ma Tar prepared to go.

'Do not stay long. There is a lot of work here. And here, take this for your mother.' Grandaunt for the first time handed out 25 kyats to Ma Tar. Ma Tar, looking for a reason to return home, left straightaway.

When she got home, she found her mother more ill than she had imagined. 'Mother, you are very ill, why did you not ask for me? It is not that I live faraway.'

'It is nothing serious. I will get better in a few days.'

But mother who had neglected her health for years and years was now afflicted with pain. She was suffering from post-menopausal symptoms and was no longer able to walk around and sell boiled peas.

This time, Ma Tar would not leave her mother's side.

* * *

One month after Ma Tar returned, mother passed away. Poverty took mother's life.

Father who had stayed leisurely his whole life had to lift up his spirit and motivate himself to work hard. Ma Tar who knew poverty but had never suffered grief was without anyone to cling to and depend on. She could not neglect her father and younger brother and go back to grand aunty's place.

Ma Tar now needed a job. But what kind of work could she take up? Father was too considerate to ask his maiden daughter to do any work. And he could not ask his only son to stop going to school, either.

Saddened and disheartened, Ma Tar wanted to find someone to rely on. She wanted someone to consult with and share her problems with. She had Thin Thin Mar and Mya Shwe around her. They were in the same boat, struggling for their lives on their own.

'How about joining me in the rice fields Ma Tar?' Thin Thin Mar said.

'Hey, she cannot work together with your parents like you do. It is not possible.' Mya Shwe objected.

'There are many paid labourer.'

'But work is not always available.'

'It cannot be helped. But if you are jobless, this kind of work is agreeable.'

'Yes, but it will be tiring.'

'Getting tired is not a novelty. It should not worry you.'

They did not take Mya Shwe's words seriously, who did not want Ma Tar to work as a paid labourer under the scorching sun.

After consulting with her father, the plan was cancelled. Ma Tar had the responsibility to cook and feed her father and younger brother. It would be necessary for the three of them to make ends meet with the money father earned.

Ma Tar did not despair. She wanted to see Win Hlaing to whom she was strongly attached. Win Hlaing was more educated than Thin Thin Mar and Mya Shwe, so she expected him to give better advice.

'Thin Thin Mar, I would like to see brother Win Hlaing.'

'Why? Are you sweethearts?'

Ma Tar's face flushed with embarrassment.

'Why, no. I have never felt that way. I just miss him.'

Thin Thin Mar laughed. 'Yes, I want to see him too. If we go up the hill, he will surely be there. We can ask Mya Shwe to take us.'

Mya Shwe came wearing a smile because they had asked for her. When they told her they wanted to go and pay homage to the pagoda on the hill, she was pleased. But Ma Tar and Thin Thin Mar had their own plans, and they looked for Win Hlaing's photo shop.

When Win Hlaing bobbed up somewhere near the Lwan Zedi, Mya Shwe realized their intention and her face became grouchy.

'Hey, what are you doing here? Have you come to worship at the pagoda?' Win Hlaing asked with excitement. He looked at them in amazement, those girls whom he had not seen for a long time. They had lost their childish looks and become relaxed and composed. Ma Tar looked more mature than her age.

'Ma Tar said she wanted to see you so I brought her,' Thin Thin Mar explained. 'What? How about you? You do not want to see me?'

Mya Shwe was looking at her two friends and their words grated upon her ears. 'As for me, I came along not to see you but because they hired my horse cart. I am anxious about my cart so I am going back down.'

'Hey wait. I will treat you at a snack bar.' Only when Win Hlaing hugged Mya Shwe by the neck and pulled her back, she softened.

Ma Tar had nothing to say to him. What could Win Hlaing do besides consoling Ma Tar for losing her mother? To help her out was not an easy task as they were all in the same boat, and still in their youth.

'The number of photographers has increased so work is getting less. I cannot buy a good camera so I have to keep using the old one. How about you Ma Tar, what are you doing now?'

'I am doing nothing. I do not know what to do.'

They had nothing special to say to each other and were just trying to cling onto friendship in the narrow confines of their world.

'You must accept my treat at the snack bar.'

They all descended the hill. Young flower sellers were calling out to them to buy their flowers but they did not buy any. They once had called out to visitors, just like those girls.

* * *

Ma Tar's resort was neither Win Hlaing nor Mya Shwe nor Thin Thin Mar. The realization dawned on her clearly now.

Win Hlaing was slinging his camera and earning his livelihood. Mya Shwe was driving her horse cart and earning her livelihood. Thin Thin Mar was working alongside her parents to earn their living.

* * *

By and by, residents of Magyeesin village heard the sweet voice of a girl known as Ma Tar calling out 'boiled peas' along the lanes of the village.

April 1981

Ma Nyo Pyar, Resident of Kawliya Streamside, Bago Region

I had not visited my village in a very long time.

To tell you the truth, ever since I passed my matriculation examination and joined Yangon University, I had quit my village.

At one time, I was among those who used to grandiloquently proclaim that the more educated youths of the village should return to their native place after receiving their education and serve with their village benevolence.

During my first days at the university, I really missed my village where I had my mother, my father, a plot of freehold land full of a variety of crops and cereals, the little stream that flowed beside our village where we used to swim and play, my buddies, and Ma Nyo Mya.

I missed my mother the most because she pampered me. Of three siblings, I was the only boy. My elder sister and younger sister had to work in the fields so they had a tanned complexion. I was different from them. I was fair. My sisters were sickly and thin. I was big, strong, and sturdy. They told me the midwife sweated all over to deliver me.

And there were words mother used to say.

'When I was pregnant with the other children, I had no cravings. With him, I craved for meat and fish, and a whole bunch of bananas had to be kept hung up. I had pleasant dreams too. Since then, I thought this one child would be exceptional.'

Contriving to boast out of nothing, that was my mother.

She let her daughters study just enough to read and write but when I got to fifth standard, she sent me to the town school three miles away, taking me with her daily when she went there to sell vegetables. That describes my beloved mother.

Mother did not talk as much as father. She was curt and did whatever was necessary.

Although father did not say so, it was apparent he had high hopes for me.

'Try to do well in your studies. Only then you will not have to toil in the fields under the sun. If you are educated you will be dignified.'

Father, like any other simple countryman, had the strong belief that if you were educated, you would not need to work in the fields.

'But Father, only if educated persons work in the fields, the local peasantry will further improve.'

At the time I had just passed the matriculation exam and I used to say grandiloquent words. Now, I remember those words only sometimes. But it seems my father did not forget my words though he never chided me for it. That describes my father.

Our plantation had a large variety of fruits and cereals, from big trees like mango and tamarind to vegetables like watercress and roselle. Seasonal fruits like marian and gourd were there too. Mother sold the produce of the plantation and bore my school expenses and also adorned and dressed up my sisters. Our small plantation supported our family's business and was a restful and pleasurable place.

My small native Baw Lel village is beside Kawliya stream. The stream supports the agriculture of the village. In a way, the stream is the main support for all the villagers. My friends and I grew up swimming and playing in the stream.

Ma Nyo Mya was my best-loved female buddy. Sprightly as a male, she did not hang out much with girls her age. Instead, she hung out with our group of boys. In climbing guava trees and tamarind trees, no one could beat Ma Nyo Mya. In catching fish and throwing a fishnet, even in driving the bullock cart, she was the fastest. Ma Nyo Mya was frank in speech and laughed heartily. She was very unladylike. She had tanned skin and stumpy legs but her eyes were clear and mesmerizing.

A lot of the young village men courted Ma Nyo Mya, but nobody dared commit physically. Due to her reputation, they were scared of her. Ma Nyo Mya and I were playmates since childhood. We swam together in the stream. Towards the end, when Ma Nyo Mya started washing clothes and bathing in front of me with her slippery longyi wrapped high over the breast, it made us realize it was time to part our ways.

Ma Nyo Mya, just like other girls in the village, left school before finishing fourth standard. As a high school student, I was popular among all the village girls. But my only interest was in my childhood buddy, Ma Nyo Mya. She was frank and friendly with me. When talking with me, she did not lower her eyelids in embarrassment like the other girls.

'Nyo Mya, when I finish my studies and return here, I will marry you. Don't you go and marry someone else. Wait for me.'

'How accommodating! But do not evade later saying Aunty Chit is not in agreement.'

Ma Nyo Mya was referring to my mother who she knew over-reacted in matters where her son was concerned.

In the end, I was among those village youths who excelled academically and got to the university. I parted from everything I held dear.

I realized only later that what I thought was 'just for a time' became 'once and for all'. Now everything including me had changed, and it had been over ten years.

Now that I have no option but to return to the village, all the things I had cherished and obsessed over have once again made me wistful and nostalgic. But what captured my senses this time was neither Ma Nyo Mya, nor my mother who passed away last year, nor Baw Lel village and its Kawliya stream.

This time what engaged me were the children who, as we had when we were young, played and gambolled near Kawliya stream. Among them, the one I was most interested in was Ma Nyo Pyar.

Yes, Ma Nyo Pyar, the young daughter of my beloved Ma Nyo Mya.

* * *

When I first got to the university, I regularly wrote to my village. I returned home during the holidays. In Yangon, I had no chance to stay at the hostel like other students. My father's first cousin brother, my uncle U Tin Hla, worked at the Kamayut vest factory. He was just an ordinary worker. I had to stay with him in the vest factory lane. It was convenient for me. I got admitted to medical college.

Later, putting the blame on voluminous studies, I no longer went back regularly to the village during the holidays. If I did go back, I could stay only for a short time. I who was village-happy

had now become city-happy. I had reason to be happy. I had
found a girl who was sweeter than Ma Nyo Mya.

War War lived at the top of our road and she was a student
at the main arts and science university. I met War War every
time I went to college. Befitting her name, she had a soft yellow
complexion. Her way of dressing was neither like a Yangon girl
nor plain like Ma Nyo Mya. To me, it was attractive. She was a
Pathein girl. A group of girls including War War had rented a
cottage at the top of the road and used it like a boarding house.
Therefore, War War and I had the chance to see each other freely.
One of the main reasons I could forget my village was War War.

I went to the village after I had completed my house
surgeon training. By this time, the condition of the village had
also improved a lot. There were graduates like me who had
returned to the village. Some stayed at the village and went to
work in the city not too far away. Some worked as clerical staff,
some became managers, some worked as school teachers. But
there was none who worked in the fields like I once said. I could
not either. I was a doctor.

'To which township did you apply for?' My laconic father
asked just that. Up to that time, I had not yet applied for a
government post. I was still mixed up and contemplating on
the future.

War War had finished university earlier than me and was
already working in Yangon. The reason she worked in Yangon
was because she did not want to be apart from me. If War War
as a girl had not returned to her parents but stayed and coped
with hardship in Yangon, would it be fair to leave her and go
back to my village? I too did not want to part from her. I had
already decided to marry War War.

'I have not applied anywhere Father. If I apply, I may not
get the township I apply for. Some are posted to far-flung

areas. In Yangon, a friend of mine has opened a clinic and has asked me to work at this clinic. I am pondering if I should,' I replied indistinctly.

Then mother who loved me dearly, interrupted.

'Oh, do not make him apply if he might get posted to a faraway place. He will be alone. We cannot leave our home and follow him. Working in Yangon will be quite nice. It is easy to go there any time.'

Our town is in Bago township so the distance from Yangon is not far. They simply thought that I still found it difficult to live away from them. It is usual for parents to care for their children however much they have grown up. Parents do not want their children to live afar. While I was at college, even though I did not return home often, mother used to visit me if her whim took her. She had noted the route from Yangon Railway Station to Kamayut. When she visited, she brought fish paste and dried fish for uncle's family. Now she had no idea that I was no longer under her care but under my beloved's tender treatment.

During my days there, I often met Ma Nyo Mya. We had always lived near the same stream and drunk the same water, so meeting her could not be avoided.

Ma Nyo Mya did not treat me as intimately as before. She still looked at me with familiarity in her eyes but she could not make out my different attitude and so she kept a distance. If I greeted her, she would happily respond.

One time, she and I met face to face. She was washing clothes in the stream alone. I went to fetch water for my folks. We had to drink water from the stream. When water ebbed away in the stream and there arose sandbanks, children dug deep in the sand and made a big open tub that held cool, clean, and clear water springing out from the sand.

I was holding two buckets and going down into the stream when Ma Nyo Mya was sitting properly on a stone slab quite near, banging and washing clothes.

Ma Nyo Mya with her longyi wrapped high up the breast was still buxom as before. The impression of her two bodice strings showed on her tanned skin as two white stripes. The upper hem cloth of her longyi was quite loose. I diverted my eyes.

'Hey, the doctor is fetching water! Your action might bring rain right in the middle of the hot season!'

Ma Nyo Mya readjusted her longyi and spoke provokingly. When we were young, we all fetched water from the stream happily. In the rainy season when rains became scarce, water from the stream had to be routed to the paddy fields.

'Is it strange for a doctor to fetch water, Ma Nyo Mya?' pretended to not understand that she was just provoking me.

'I do not know. Your mother was saying her son will be opening a big clinic in Yangon and practising there. She often repeats that her son has been special since his childhood, so he is destined to have a good future elsewhere rather than being bound to the village. Just imagine, who would forcefully keep her son tied down to the village? It will also not be difficult for us to match up with doctors if we go to the city.'

I knew very well that Ma Nyo Mya was assailing me while she had the chance. But her reproving words no longer moved me. I just laughed aloud.

'Mother is just boasting about her son as usual Ma Nyo Mya. Forbear her.'

'Of course, her son is worth boasting now.'

I was the target of her words.

'I have not forgotten my village or my village buddies. Working in Yangon will be only for a short time. It is just a suitable alternative.' I gave a lame excuse. I then put down my two buckets and sat down near her.

'Am I among the village buddies you mentioned?' Ma Nyo Mya asked so bluntly, I was abashed. It seemed she had not forgotten the words I had once told her.

Village girls marry young but Ma Nyo Mya was still single. I knew very well that there were several men who wanted to marry her.

'Of course, you are.' I avoided Ma Nyo Mya's glaring eyes and responded furtively.

'Well, nice to be in it. I never forget the words I have been told. My mother wants to marry me off to Ko Aye Maung. Their folks are influential in the village and your mother is a good go-between. Guess she wants to save you from my clutches!'

I could no longer ignore Ma Nyo Mya's frank words. 'Aye Maung is good-hearted and he works industriously. Not a bad match.'

Aye Maung was in the same class with me up to seventh standard. His father was a village elder.

'Ko Aung Khaing, do you agree with the match?'

I dared not listen to her trembling voice. Neither did I dare to look into her eyes which would be beaming and moistened. I just nodded my head.

'Hey, there is a lot of drinking water at home. This one haul is enough!'

My mother called out from the precipice. I left quickly after taking leave from Ma Nyo Mya. My buckets were not half-filled with water.

The sound of Ma Nyo Mya washing the clothes with a deliberate bang echoed across the streamside.

* * *

'It is necessary to go to the district for one or two years, my love. Only afterwards, they can try and get me transferred to Yangon. So, I guess I will have to forbear the two years and go there, do you not think so?'

After War War and I got married, we managed to scrape our living in Yangon. We had to manage our budget with the money I earned from the clinic and the money War War earned from her work. Our parents were not well-off to make things easier for us, so we had to struggle on our own. We had to work very hard to keep up with the living expenses of city life. It was not easy for an ordinary doctor to earn alongside specialist doctors in the city. So, we had to look for another way.

War War said she would try to go to the district and get transferred back to Yangon in two years' time.

'Good. It is convenient as I want to return to my village. Let us apply with my town as priority.'

'But your town is too backward. Let us apply to my town. My father will arrange everything for you to open a clinic there.'

I always followed my beloved wife War War's advice. Now I was a bit hesitant, so she said provoking words.

'Why, love, is it because you want to meet up with your old flame?'

'She is married and has her own family, War War.'

Not long after War War and I got married, Ma Nyo Mya wedded Ko Aye Maung.

'If I cannot get transferred back to Yangon in two- or three-years' time, we will transfer to my town.'

War War reasoned that if we transferred to her town, we would be saving on living expenses. Also, her parents would arrange for my clinic, so we would be saving all that we earned. Since it was my duty to give preference to my wife's words, I had to agree. My father had no other interest besides his paddy field and he would not arrange a clinic for me. Actually, father was fed up with me.

We still had no offspring. War War was not ready yet. When I went to the district, War War would stay at a relative's place. Both of us could save up and when we got back to Yangon, we would get ourselves a moderate place to live in with the money we had saved. Then, I would be able to call up my mother and she could travel between Yangon and her home. Now our place was so narrow that we could not even call up mother should she need to receive some kind of medical treatment in Yangon.

These were our plans.

But mother passed away while I was in Pathein. Just like people who do not know what they have got until it is gone, I lamented the loss of my mother only after she was gone.

'In the town there are quite a lot of doctors who come up from Yangon to open clinics here but at the general hospital, there is only one physician and when he is away, there is no substitute.'

Mother who was afraid of hospitals agreed to be sent to a hospital only when the pain became unbearable. At the time, the physician was not there. She needed an operation so she had to be sent to a hospital quite far from our town. On the way, mother passed away.

I could not face the disdainful looks the whole village gave me. Father with cold eyes, Ma Nyo Mya with bright but estranged eyes.

'War War, I will have to move to my hometown. Your town is big and they have a lot of physicians whereas there is only one hospital and one physician in our town. The physician cannot cope and an assistant has been requested for quite some time. Do not stop me this time.'

Now, only I could utter decisive words.

But mother who contrived to boast proudly about me was no more . . .

* * *

I got to stay at a cool quiet cottage in the hospital compound. Father did not even consider leaving his house and field to join me at my place. I had to visit him on and off. But I was hardly free to do so. I struggled with the patients that arrived from various townships. Urgent cases, which needed better medical equipment, had to be referred to other town hospitals. For me, it was like repaying a debt of gratitude to the country. Our province consisted mostly of peasants. Whether young or old, they all worked as paddy growers. The number of village youths who joined the university were increasing but, compared to its population, the ratio was low. This made me recall the grandiloquent catch-words I had said at one time.

While I was gazing into the dark and silent hospital compound, I saw some lights coming towards me from the hospital entrance lane. I glanced at the clock. It was after 10 p.m. These past one or two days, there had been electricity cut-offs so the whole town was dark. The hospital compound was dark too.

I peered towards the lane and saw two sidecars entering. It must be a patient in urgent need of treatment. I put on a sweater and walked towards the hospital. I saw the door to the physician's house being opened too.

The sidecars stopped in front of the hospital. I walked with haste. I saw the patient being carried down from the sidecar. When I reached the hospital, the patient was already on the examination table. I stepped forward making the people around the patient disperse.

'What's wrong?'

'Snakebite.'

I took the lantern from the hospital guard and looked at the patient. It was Aye Maung, Ma Nyo Mya's husband. When I looked sideways, I saw Ma Nyo Mya who had on her head a towel-turban, crying and sobbing.

'Do not tell me he has died, Ko Aung Khaing!'

The usually bright eyes of Ma Nyo Mya's were languid with anxiety. The physician entered and we made way for him. We assisted him in every way we could. At the start of the rainy season, it was not unusual for farmers to be bitten by poisonous snakes. Therefore, we had to keep ready the necessary drugs and medicines for treatment.

'Ma Nyo Mya, he is lucky. It is not fatal. He was stunned due to shock. Did you catch the snake?'

A knowledgeable villager who had killed and brought the snake, showed it to the doctors. The wound was also bound up in a tourniquet as it was advantageous to the patient.

In the morning, Ma Nyo Mya and her companions from the village went back. The patient was safe now. He was dozing in bed. Ma Nyo Mya had looked at me with her glistening eyes. I did not sleep the whole night but stayed and waited near them.

'Thank you so much Ko Aung Khaing. I really mean it. Although I brought him to the hospital, I had no hope thinking if the physician is not around, we might have to give up.'

The other villagers also looked at me with gratitude. I did not know them well but I knew that all of them had connections with our village.

'We heard that one of our villagers is a doctor here but it is only now that we get to see you.'

'Hey, it is Aunty Chit's son. Oh, how I miss Aunty Chit. If Ko Aung Khaing was here with her, Aunty Chit would not have died.'

Ma Nyo Mya with teary eyes pined for my mother who did not want her for a daughter-in- law. In my heart, there arose a deep sharp pain.

Ma Nyo Mya and villagers went back. I told them to leave the patient at the hospital.

When they left, I walked back to my little cottage.

The cottage with no mistress was disorderly and messed up. Making a cup of coffee for myself, I thought of writing to War War. I must tell her to quit her job, which paid only 300 kyats—just enough to buy a bateik longyi—and come stay with me.

I no longer felt like leaving my native place. I had more debts of gratitude to repay.

* * *

'Hey friend, you are already eating rice and all!'

On hearing my voice, Aye Maung looked up with pleasure.

'Yes, I am so glad Aung Khaing Nyo Mya told me this morning and I am so grateful to you. I can be discharged this afternoon?'

'Do not rush, my friend. Your wound is quite deep.'

I stopped my words there. The wound in the ankle also touched the bone. He would not yet be able to step well.

Just then, a little girl came into the room holding a water bottle. 'Have you had enough, Father? Take some more and eat.'

I assessed the girl with locks of hair gathered atop and tied in a tuft. 'Ma Nyo Mya'. I said the name softly. How she resembled Ma Nyo Mya. Bright eyes, tanned skin, buxom figure, age around ten and a dasher like Ma Nyo Mya when she was young.

'Is she your daughter?'

'Yes friend. Because I am absent, Nyo Mya has to work in the fields so she sent her daughter. Here, daughter, this is our friend from our village. Now he is a doctor.'

The girl put the water bottle on the table and looked at me with a smile. The sweetness of her face did not resemble her mother.

'I know, Father. Mother told me the doctor and she were childhood friends and that the doctor is a kind and generous person.'

Her words almost made Aye Maung lose his composure but he instantly controlled himself.

'My daughter is a dasher. How about you? How many children do you have?'

Aye Maung, a countryman, was treating me frankly and with familiarity, but his daughter looked embarrassed in case her father might be offending me, so she kept looking at her father. The girl seemed to be a shrewd child.

'I do not have any. Well, father and daughter, you stay here. I will go on a round to see other patients.'

'Yes doctor,' the girl replied briskly.

I came out. The face of Ma Nyo Mya's daughter was imprinted firmly in my mind. Such a sweet girl!

The next day I could not see Aye Maung and his daughter. I was in the infectious disease prevention programme, touring other villages. When I returned, I learnt that Aye Maung had been discharged.

In the evening, I was asleep with fatigue when I heard some voices in front of the house. 'I heard the doctor has come back, and I have come to pay respect to him.'

I heard a girl and my helper speaking.

'You can leave the gift behind. I will tell the doctor when he wakes up.'

'My mother asked me to see the doctor personally and give it to him.'

The girl and my helper were talking to each other so I got up from the bed. As I had thought, it was Ma Nyo Mya's young daughter.

'Come Daughter, please enter.'

I felt satisfied for having addressed her as daughter. I too should have had sons and daughters by this time.

The girl turned from my helper and entered boldly. In her hand was a basket full of fruits and vegetables.

'Father is now home, Doctor. This morning, mother came along too. You were not there, and we learnt that you will be back this evening so mother sent me with these. Both father and mother asked me to invite you to come visit the village.'

Saying so, the girl sat down on the floor and paid obeisance to me. I did not know how to give blessings.

'How old are you, Daughter?'

'Nine years.'

'And what is your name?'

'It is Ma Nyo Pyar.'

When we were young, we used to affectionately call Ma Nyo Mya 'Nyo Pyar Nyet', meant (brownish, smooth, and delicate complexion). Ma Nyo Mya seemed to be fond of that name.

'Your mother is a good name-giver. Do you go to school?'

'Yes, Doctor.'

'In which standard are you?'

'Third standard.'

'You are clever. Ask your mother to let you study up to tenth standard and send you to university after you pass the matriculation examination. Tell your mother I said so.'

Imbued with the attitude of an educated person, I advised her.

'I want to do it Doctor but our village-school has classes up to fourth standard only. Mother would not let me come up to town to study.'

'Hey, it is not that far. I will tell your mother. You can come, can you not?'

'Yes. I can. I am used to coming here every morning.'

'Really? What do you come here for?'

'To sell vegetables.'

I suddenly remembered my mother who used to come to town to sell vegetables. Starting from early dawn, she and I walked along the motorway to town. And that was how I passed the matriculation examination.

'Okay, I will tell your mother. You are only in third standard so it is still a bit too soon.'

'Yes, please tell her, Uncle doctor. I am leaving now. I came along with other villagers who were coming this way.'

'Yes, yes, go back. The vegetables are abundant. But there is no one to cook those for me.'

Ma Nyo Pyar cast her eyes around. 'Where is Uncle doctor's wife?'

'She is in Yangon.'

'Oh, my mother did not come along because she thought Uncle's wife must be here.'

This time, the one to lose composure was me. The girl realized she had uttered inappropriate words so she flitted her tongue and lowered her head. 'Go back now before it is dark.' The girl left.

Looking at the back of Ma Nyo Mya's daughter, Ma Nyo Pyar, I sighed imperceptibly. The girl was smart and seemed intelligent. Her mother, Ma Nyo Mya, was sharp and bright too but she did not have the chance to study up to high school. Now, her daughter, Ma Nyo Pyar, seemed to have the same fate. Perhaps, she too would have to leave school and work in the fields before completing fourth standard. If she had rich and modern parents from the city, she would receive higher education and mingle with the upper class.

Some children were running around and playing in the compound. They belonged to families that had come to the hospital to tend to patients who were family members. It was inevitable that the children had to be brought along too.

* * *

'What went wrong, love? I have been anxious since last week when you did not return.'

My wife complained as soon as she arrived. She had come because I had sent for her urgently. Usually, on holidays or on days I was free, I went to Yangon to meet War War.

'Nothing wrong, War War. Please be seated calmly. I have so many things to tell you.'

War War scanned and gauged the whole place and heaved a sigh furtively. With the mistress of the house, my little cottage would look spick and span.

'This time I have to tell you decisively, War War. Two of us living apart has no meaning. And doing this because of your master plan has brought us closer to nowhere! Instead of saving enough to be able to live together, we have to be live apart which is more costly, is it not so?'

'Well, it is because you are not saving up. And you refuse to open a clinic. In Pathein, we could save some.'

'And those savings have been almost entirely spent on moving expenses, War War. I could save up but you could not save up either in Yangon and your parents even had to send you money. Opening a clinic here is not at all possible. The physician and I, both of us have to work round the clock. Only doctors from Yangon can come and open clinics here. And even then, for difficult cases, they have to rely on the hospital.'

'It was you who said you so very much wanted to move here.'

'Yes, and I already explained the reason.'

'And what do you want now?'

'I want you to quit your job and move here. Or, you can take up a job here.'

'No, no. I do not want to settle anywhere other than my native place.'

I had acquired a strong will to fight for my wish. My wife of course was still refusing doggedly.

But soon afterwards, I had my wish. I stayed away from Yangon for long periods so War War had to come visiting. My little cottage became a cottage for the two of us. War War came to love the place and she furnished and decorated it to her heart's desire. In the end, she took long leave from work and came to stay. I tried to win her over to leave her job once and for all.

The head physician moved away so I had to take his place. War War became 'the physician's wife', respected by everyone. She became attached to the provincial villagers who treated her with respect. In the end, War War decided to come and stay beside me. Another reason was because we were going to have what we needed for our family. War War was expecting.

* * *

Now I visited the village quite often. If I did not go, father would drop in to see us when he came to town to sell beans and rice. He began to show his forgiveness by gesture.

Whenever I went to the village, I visited Ma Nyo Mya's place.

Aye Maung as well as Ma Nyo Mya and their young daughter Ma Nyo Pyar welcomed me with open arms. One sad thing was, because of the snake bite, Aye Maung's leg went lame.

It was fortunate that Ma Nyo Mya was capable of coping as a leader. I learnt that besides Ma Nyo Pyar, they had two other children.

I grew quite interested in Ma Nyo Pyar. She had passed fourth standard. I decided to tell her parents to continue with her schooling.

At first, Ma Nyo Mya was disinclined.

'She happens to be the eldest, Ko Aung Khaing. She knows how to sell. And we depend on her for cooking and looking after the younger ones.'

'But do not look at it from an angle of convenience, Ma Nyo Mya. You have the duty to open avenues for her future.'

'Yes, it's true. When I was young, I wanted to attend school like you all but my mother did not let me.'

'That is what I mean Ma Nyo Mya.'

I talked to her seriously so she responded with weal. But Ma Nyo Mya was mixed-up.

Aye Maung did not say a word. He was feeling down.

'Daughter, do you want to go to school in town?' Ma Nyo Mya asked her daughter.

'I want to, Mother. Uncle doctor said I can stay at his place and go to school. He told me he would help me study until I become a doctor.'

Ma Nyo Pyar told her mother the words I had taught her. Both Ma Nyo Mya and Aye Maung looked at me.

'We thank you Aung Khaing. We live a hand to mouth existence, and we cannot afford that much. We have to consider the younger ones too.'

Ma Nyo Mya was watching me with emotion.

'A girl does not need that much education, Ko Aung Khaing. If she passes ninth or tenth standard she can become a teacher—that will be enough. Even that is indulging her wish. Otherwise, we will just make her work in the field. We had to work like that when we were young.'

'But times have changed, Ma Nyo Mya.'

Although I said it, even extracting one Ma Nyo Pyar out of the many village children proved to be hard.

'Well, she can stay with you if she wants to. Your wife is here too, is not she, Ko Aung Khaing?'

'Yes, we have no children. War War will love her at sight. My wife has no companion. And if your daughter has to go to school from here, it will not be easy for a girl. That is why we want to make her stay with us. She can come back to the village on school holidays.'

In the end, Ma Nyo Mya and her husband agreed to the plan hesitatingly. I felt proud for having done a service to them. I thought to myself that though oil cannot be made from one sesamum seed, but sowing a good seed is no less beneficial. I had the desire to create educated youths from these paddy fields.

* * *

'Now you have a companion, War War.'

War War and I had discussed previously about Ma Nyo Pyar. It was not too easy but not a knotty problem either.

Ma Nyo Pyar arrived looking neat and tidy with a bedroll and a bundle of clothes. She also brought the rice, cooking oil, and fish paste that her mother had sent. I could not but feel respect for Ma Nyo Mya's pride.

'Hmm, at least she looks pretty and smart.' War War made a non-committal remark.

'Well girl, your duty is to go to school regularly and study hard. In your free time, if uncle is not here, you will be my companion and also help around the house. That is all. But you must keep yourself neat and tidy at all times.'

War War gave me an appraising glance. 'Tell me love, do I have to address her as daughter?'

'As you wish, War War. Well girl, the room over there is yours. There is a writing table too. In the morning, I will take you to school.'

Ma Nyo Pyar lowered her head before us and went into the room. I did not like War War's behaviour on Ma Nyo Pyar's arrival, so I stayed silent.

'Maung Thaung, put away those things.'

War War tilted up her chin at the things Ma Nyo Pyar had brought and told the helper to put them away. Then she went into the room.

I remained alone and pondered if my action had been somewhat aggravating.

* * *

'A, one thing, one animal, one person. C-a-t cat, r-a-t rat, b-a-t bat . . . '

When I returned from the hospital and heard Ma Nyo Pyar's voice learning out loud, I was delighted. When she heard my footsteps, she came running out. She took the things I was carrying and put them away neatly.

'Uncle doctor, look at me. I have had a haircut!'

'Wow! Who did it for you? Was it Aunty War War?'

'No, Uncle.'

Ma Nyo Pyar glanced at Maung Thaung who was standing close by. Maung Thaung was grinning.

'My handiwork, Boss. Is it not nice?'

It was then that I took a good look at the girl. The original hairdo which was a top knot with a circular fringe was gone. Maung Thaung had turned it into a hairstyle that looked more like half a shell of a coconut.

'Why did you do it? She looked nice with her original hairdo!'

'Aunty War War made him do it, Uncle.'

'She had to have it cut. Such a lot of lice in her hair!' War War called out from the room.

'Well, go and have it beautified at the hair salon tomorrow. Now, uncle is hungry. Maung Thaung, prepare dinner.'

I argued no more with War War. 'Well War War, let us have dinner.'

'I have finished eating, Love.'

Usually, War War waited to have dinner with me. Yesterday, I happened to ask Ma Nyo Pyar to join us. The girl washed her hands perfunctorily and came to the table. Upon seeing War War wrinkle her nose in distaste, I looked at the girl's hands.

'Girl, wash your hands thoroughly with soap. And cut your fingernails. In future, do not eat with unclean hands. But for now, you can use spoon and fork to eat.'

Ma Nyo Pyar did not seem to enjoy her food because she had to use a spoon and fork like us. As villagers, we too felt satiated only if we ate with our hands. In the fields, after picking groundnuts and chillies, we just brushed one hand against the other and washed with water before eating. Now, we had to teach Ma Nyo Pyar to live and eat healthily.

Today, I sat alone at the table.

'Girl, why do you not come and eat with me?'

'I have finished eating, Uncle.'

'With whom? With Aunty War War?'

'No, Uncle. With Uncle Ko Maung Thaung.'

'Okay then, go and study.'

Ma Nyo Pyar remained standing near me, covertly. I glanced at her thinking perhaps she wanted to say something. Her eyes were wet and bright.

'What, girl? What do you want to say?'

'Uncle, the day after tomorrow is school holiday. So, may I go back to my village tomorrow evening?'

'Hmm, it has been only a short while since you started school, but already you are missing your home? If there is a chance traveller tomorrow, you may go along. But you must come back in time for school.'

'Certainly, Uncle.'

I noticed Ma Nyo Pyar's different behaviour but I did not enquire.

Ma Nyo Pyar had tenacity. And she was eager for education. Although I worried in case, she did not return because of War War's treatment of her, she came back regularly every week. And, she had a good bent of mind too. Just as she did not tell on us to her folks, she did not tell on her folks to us. Because of Ma Nyo Pyar's shrewdness, War War's attitude towards her changed gradually.

'Here, your daughter is proudly saying that she stood fifth in the monthly exam.'

'Really, show me.'

Ma Nyo Pyar was proudly showing off the report card from school.

'English 50, good, Maths 80, not bad. If you study harder than this, you will stand first in no time.'

'You Baw Lel locals are clever, hmm.' War War made fun of her husband.

'War War, there are many clever persons everywhere. Only thing is, they do not get the chance to prove it.'

'So that is why you are trying to polish a diamond in the rough, ha ha.'

Despite my wife making fun of me, I was proud of my action. If my mother had not brought me to school while she peddled vegetables in town, I would never have become a doctor. Even if Ma Nyo Pyar did not become a doctor, I would be satisfied if she became a teacher like her mother said.

After staying with us for some time, Ma Nyo Pyar was good as gold. Because of War War's discipline, she became meticulous about cleanliness, and she also helped around the house. When I went on field trips, she was War War's good companion. She was helpful in every possible way to War War who was heavy with child. And she did not fail to study her lessons.

Sending her to school was not our completely responsibility. We only had to bear the expenses for books and clothes. On the way back from her weekly visits, her mother usually sent her with food and pocket money.

When her final exam drew near, we did not allow her to go back to the village. We made her study at home, so she had a sad look.

'Ma Nyo Pyar, you can ask me for whatever you need from the village. I am going there. You have to stay at home and study since your exam is drawing near.'

Ma Nyo Pyar nodded her head apathetically.

I went alone to the village as I had not visited for some time. First, I stopped at my father's place. He was still working in the fields with fellow farmers and helpers.

'By the way, I must tell you. I heard that you are sending Ma Nyo Mya's young daughter to school.'

'Yes, Father. The girl is brilliant. It is worth doing.' I said it proudly, but I knew that if father started a conversation, there must be a reason and that perhaps it was not to praise me.

'You are saying it is worth sending her to school but here, Ma Nyo Mya and husband are tiring themselves out.'

'Why Father, how can sending this one girl to school impinge on them?'

'Hey, this girl is a reliable one. The rest are just tiny tots. Aye Maung is lame, Ma Nyo Mya has to divide her time between working in the fields and cooking for the family. The children are neglected and they look like waifs and strays.'

I remembered Ma Nyo Pyar's younger siblings. They must be of schooling age too. Father continued. 'You could attend school but your elder and younger sisters did not have the chance. It is obligatory for children of farmers to work in the fields. Only few can stay away from the fields. Just because you became a doctor, do you think it is possible for others to become doctors?'

It was lucky that my father, usually a laconic person, stopped there.

I gave him the medicines I had brought for him and left. Although I did not feel like visiting Ma Nyo Mya's place, I had to drop in.

The vegetables in the market-garden were verdant but the family had a lacklustre appearance. Aye Maung was carrying a bundle of straw with difficulty. Ma Nyo Mya had gone thin with dark, dry skin. The two pant-less children were playing in front of the house. Looking closely, I noticed Ma Nyo Mya's bulging belly. How they can breed, I said to myself!

My wife, a good planner, started a family only after ten years! Ma Nyo Mya who married later than me already had three children!

'Have you not brought along my daughter, Ko Aung Khaing?' Ma Nyo Mya greeted me and asked.

'No, the exam is drawing close so we have asked her to study at home.' 'Oh,' Ma Nyo Mya's voice was not too enthusiastic.

'Your daughter is clever. She also behaves well.'

'Yes, we have to depend on her. When she comes back, she washes all the clothes and works in the market-garden too. The load for one week.'

I thought of Ma Nyo Pyar who did not want to miss her weekly visits to the village weekly.

'The exam will be over soon.'

'Well, it had better be over. Last year, paddy did not turn out well, chilli price went down so we had a difficult time. On top of that, Ko Aye Mayng had a snakebite. What a struggle it was!'

'Nyo Mya, what are you telling the guest? Why do you not prepare some plain green tea.' Ko Aye Maung said to his wife as he climbed up the stairs slowly.

'Do not bother. I am leaving now. What do you want me to say to your daughter?'

'I would like to send some sticky rice grain and pocket money.'

Ma Nyo Mya got up to go to the part of the house where the altar was. There, in vertical position was a bamboo piggy bank. I recalled my mother saving coins in a bamboo piggy bank when she was alive.

I realized that Ma Nyo Mya was supporting her daughter not because she could afford it but because she did not want the girl to lose face.

'Never mind. No need to give her. We are giving her pocket money. She does not need any.' I left in a hurry.

I rode the bicycle along the precipice. In the stream, the water was drying out. Handmade water holes were becoming visible. School children were running out of the rundown primary school with decaying walls. Behind them was the tired-looking schoolmaster. I got down from the bicycle to greet the master. It was not the master who taught us when we were children. But he was not different from the previous one, dark-skinned with worn-out clothes. Likewise, the students were unkempt with running noses.

'Oh, here you are, Doctor. I need to let you know something. Water is becoming scarce so there is danger of a cholera outbreak. We heard the other day of some mishap in the western part.'

'Really? I will come down with my team, Master.'

'Please do it.' I left. Although I intended to remind them to drink boiled water, I did not. The children held on to the rear of my bicycle and followed shouting 'hey'. In my mind, I was hearing someone asking me 'Well, Doctor, how many more doctors do you expect to churn out from among our villagers?'

* * *

'Take a look, Love. The baby is fair-skinned. He resembles you. How big the ears are! It means he will be bright. He is the only child so we must bring him up with care.'

War War presumed our son to be the only child. It was probable. We were in no mood for more children at our age. The baby was fair just like War War said. We had planned well for this child so we had everything of necessity for him. And we were ready to provide further necessities too.

'Your son is sure to become a doctor like you. He has a wide forehead!'

'Among the children who play around in the streams, there are those with wide foreheads too. It is not at all a predictive feature!'

I understood a mother's over-reaction but I had my own painful feelings so I told her off.

'Love, what is wrong with you? It is true the wide forehead is not a predictive feature but if the child has folks to support him and improvise upon the situation, there is a high probability. We are ready to do that, are we not?'

'Yes, what I mean is, to support and improvise, there must be affordability.'

'You are talking about Ma Nyo Pyar, are you not? You have done what you wanted. What more can you do?'

I had asked Ma Nyo Pyar to come back in time for the reopening of her school. They had only sat for the first trial exam so they were allowed only ten days' holiday. Now school had restarted three days ago but Ma Nyo Pyar was nowhere to be seen.

I had urgent patients so I could not go to the village. Just the other day, I met her class teacher and she made a remark.

'Your daughter is very smart. She stood first in class. She scored full marks in Maths and the highest marks in English.'

Most people thought Ma Nyo Pyar was my adopted daughter. In the school register too, I had signed as her guardian.

If her performance continued like this, she would surely pass each academic year. I was sure of Ma Nyo Pyar's ability.

I waited one week but there was no sign of Ma Nyo Pyar so I prepared to go to the village.

'Are you going to the village, Love? Please bring back Ma Nyo Pyar.'

I did not know if my wife was feigning; I nodded my head. But it was evident that War War had grown to like Ma Nyo Pyar who would put down her schoolbag after returning from school and do the housework first.

When I got to the village, I did not see Ma Nyo Pyar. Her mother Ma Nyo Mya was not there either. Only Aye Maung and the two kids were there.

'Mother and daughter have gone to reap paddy,' Aye Maung told me. 'School has re-started. Why are you making her work there?'

'She is indispensable, Aung Khaing. I cannot work in the fields and her mother is heavy with child.'

I clicked my tongue in my mind. I went to father's place too but I did not talk about it. I just told Aye Maung to send Ma Nyo Pyar over to me.

She returned four or five days later. Her skin had become deeply tanned. The colour of her clothes had worn off. I quickly sent her off to school fearing she might be behind her lessons. But Ma Nyo Pyar was no longer ardent and enthusiastic about going to school or studying her lessons.

* * *

'Love, this time when the transfer orders come out, it will be a Yangon posting; my uncle wrote to me.' War War told me fervently. I was not too delighted. To be frank, I too wanted to stay in Yangon. I wanted to work in hospitals fully equipped with medicines and medical appliances. I wanted to take a shot at better opportunities. Some of my doctor friends had already been abroad at least two or three times. But the sentimental love for my native land had begun to take root.

'Well, transfer is good but I want to stay here one or two more years. If they do not want two doctors in the same town, then it should be somewhere near.'

'Aww, now you are having regional bias! There will be other doctors to take your place.'

'That is true.'

'By the way, if we move, it will be difficult for Ma Nyo Pyar to attend school. Let us take her to Yangon. Why do you not talk to her parents?'

Ma Nyo Pyar had gone back to her village after the final examination. Whether she would continue her schooling the next year was not certain. It was a long holiday so I refrained from saying anything yet. Only when the school reopened, would I persuade the parents into letting her study further.

It was certain Ma Nyo Pyar would not continue to go to school if I was not in this town. 'It will be good if her parents agree. The girl will be an outstanding student.' War War's expectation turned out to be true. Before long, I received transfer orders to a suburban hospital in Yangon. War War was delighted. I went to the village to tell my father about it.

'Hey Doctor, your daughter has passed the exam. Do you know about it?'

A teacher I met on the way gave me the news. I did not know about it. I just nodded my head. I was happy but not whole heartedly. This success would not change her life. It was not sufficient for her future. There were plenty of villagers who had completed seventh or eighth standard and were working in the fields. Those who had passed ninth or tenth standard worked in town as clerical staff. Some were just employed as office help or security staff. When the salary was not sufficient, they returned to work in the fields to grow chilli and groundnut. They were caught in a vicious circle.

I walked along the stream. The sandy shore was waiting for the rain. If there was rain and the stream flowed, we usually were overjoyed. While attending university in Yangon, when I gazed at Inya Lake, I forgot the stream in my village. Now that I remembered, the flow of the stream was unchanged. It was doing its bounden duty of flowing.

Now I could see the village towered by trees. There were one or two circular pools formed by the stream and some children were swimming and playing there. One girl was washing clothes on a stone slab. On a closet look, it turned out to be Ma Nyo Pyar.

'Hey, Nyo Pyar. You passed the exam. Did you know already?'

'Oh Uncle doctor, mother has given birth. Do you know?'

Our two voices came out at the same time. Ma Nyo Pyar did not seem to be affected by the good news I brought her, and I had no reason to be moved by the news she told me. I could see that the clothes she was washing were her mother's and pasoe pieces used as diapers for the baby.

'I know I have passed, Uncle. Yesterday Bo Bo came and gave me the news.'

Bo Bo was my nephew, my elder sister's son. My sister got married to a worker from a rice mill and lived in town.

Ma Nyo Pyar finished washing and came up the precipice. Her longyi tied above the breast was slightly loose.

Ma Nyo Pyar ran in front to tell her mother I was coming.

Ma Nyo Mya with a new born baby was yellow with the turmeric cream she had applied on her body. Aye Maung was watering the chilli seedlings.

'Have you come to tell us that Nyo Pyar has passed the exam, Ko Aung Khaing?' Ma Nyo Mya's voice sounded restrained.

'The middle one Aung Ngwe will go up to second standard this year. I have thought of sending him to town school.' Ma Nyo Mya's words stopped there. I did not say anything. Ma Nyo Pyar was carrying her youngest brother with tenderness.

Ma Nyo Mya looked at me diffidently. 'It's not that I do not want to have her educated because she is a girl, Ko Aung Khaing, but she is indispensable. Last year, our vegetable produce could not be sold because she was not here. Next month, the chilli seedlings will have to be sown.'

I did not utter a word. I never told her I was being transferred to Yangon or that we wanted to take Ma Nyo Pyar with us.

When I left the village to return home, children were merrily playing in a circular patterned stream pool which was just big enough for a buffalo to wallow in.

* * *

It was a misty morning. For the second time, I prepared to leave my village. I paid respect to my father and walked alone along the village stream. Last time, I had departed with high hopes. When I returned, my mother was no more. The next time I return, would I still have the chance to see my aging father?

Last time, I had to leave Ma Nyo Mya. This time I have to leave her daughter, Ma Nyo Pyar. When I return next time, will the girl be greeting me with her children just like her mother? And Ma Nyo Pyar's children, will they attend the village school off and on and play merrily in the stream pool?

If all these children no longer lived there with savoir-faire, farm lands and streams—would they silt up? Paddy and crops, would they lie dormant?

When I looked back at the village from the motorway, I saw a group of old women and young girls walking in my direction, each with a basket on her head. Like my mother, they were walking to town to sell fresh produce from their own gardens.

It was almost certain that Ma Nyo Pyar, the sweet little girl I love, would be in this group.

May 1981

Yi Yi Mar, Resident of Twelve Apartment Complex, Yankin

'One phone call will do it and yet you are making it difficult, Father!'

Daughter Yi Yi Mar was expressing her dissatisfaction with her father. These days, Yi Yi Mar said the same words again and again. So, her mother Daw Thin Kyi could no longer ignore the issue. Although respectful and afraid of her husband, she interjected in a soft tone.

'Yes, why not, Love? Our daughter is eager to work and that is why she is asking you. And it is not that difficult, is it?'

However much the words were spoken with care, a woman is a woman and there was a hint of blame in her tone. U Thaung Ngwe realized it immediately. As a father, he could forgive a daughter but he wanted to scold the wife for interfering without understanding the real situation. Lately, U Thaung Ngwe bawled at his wife whenever he was disgruntled.

'You all just talk easily. True it will not be difficult to do it but it will be like taking advantage. If you want a job, apply for it like all others, take the exam and if you get selected, then do the job. While all others are doing it this way, would it be fair for me to ask for a job for my daughter using my name? I have not gained this position by taking advantage. I earned my name because I have lived life selflessly in the service of others.'

Mother and daughter both grimaced. Daw Thin Kyi did it surreptitiously but Yi Yi Mar did it to her father's face peevishly.

'Because you lived your whole life like that, I am now asking you to put in a good word for me, Father. It is not often that you are asking for favours!' Yi Yi Mar said coaxingly.

'Favours, she said!' U Thaung Ngwe whispered to himself in a hushed tone. How come his daughter at this age already knew how to use the word 'favour'? It was used plentifully in their own times but as something to be loathed and abhorred. They had convinced the opportunists that actions done with deep conviction could win in any situation. Now, his daughter did not see 'favour' as something to be loathed. She was sweetly urging him to ask for it just one time.

Well, there is that 'one' time for everyone. But it is best if that one time never crops up. Would it be proper to demolish his cherished principles with that one request for favour?

'Be patient, Daughter. You will achieve something in the course of time.' He consoled his daughter in his softest tone. As he aged, he had come to accept the theory that if something was bound to happen, it would. But just like his daughter, in his youth there were times when he was overly and unduly eager. Yi Yi Mar was still young. Seventeen years was very young, but she kept insisting that she wanted to work. Did it not speak of her enthusiasm? He himself had to struggle at about her age. In deep poverty, he had to build his own life. And later, he toiled for the country.

'It is the beginning of term so there are still fewer lessons to be learned, Father. If I take up a job, it will not be proper to apply for leave after only a short service. Leave will have to be taken for the final examination. That is why I want to join early. I have passed the written exam, and it would be a pity if I do not get the job. My friends tell me that no matter how good my marks were in the written exam, they will not count in the interview. Last time I was left out just like that.'

How could he change his daughter's views? Perhaps, he was behind the times. It was true that the procedures of his times were sometimes no longer in tune with the present ones. But that was no reason to discard his beliefs. Beliefs are beliefs. Water can be mixed with other substances to drink but the basis is water itself.

'It is not proper that one can get a job only as a favour. At work, you will be scorned by others for securing the job through a person who dispensed favour. The proper way to get a job is through your own effort.'

In his daughter's youthful life experience, he did not want her to forget that personal integrity was the best ability. If she thought that ability was not necessary to get a job, would not she be in dire straits?

'But Father, if there are several persons with the same qualifications, what to do? Just like you Father, you have the ability but others have better positions. Can anyone say it is because you have no ability? You are complacent because you are an adult. I have never had a job so I want it badly.'

He liked the way his daughter put it. But he did not like the part about being complacent because he was an adult. He wanted to tell her that when he was young too, he had to be complacent with the way things were. He had said it often. Perhaps, repetition made his words ineffective. The moment he started with 'In our days . . . ', the children would turn the other way. He might be laughed at but who could argue that in his repetitive words lay the country's historical struggles, in which he too had participated.

'Some people know what I did for the country at one time. I accepted the job because they offered it to me. It is my dignity, Daughter. I would rather perish than dishonour my principles.'

This time, Daw Thin Kyi's grimace was discernible. Although she dared not to interfere, her growing unease was recognizable.

'For you it is true,' she voiced it anyway.

'Well, my Daughter is starting on her journey only now. If my help is needed, I would have to do it.'

Yi Yi Mar was joyous. Getting this much compliance from her father was enough for her. She knew that it was imperative for her to get her father's support.

* * *

It could be said that Daw Thin Kyi was narrow-minded because she was a woman but it was also true that she could not be conventional in all matters like her husband. Daw Thin Kyi had put up with the restrictions of being a politician's wife. Let alone the discreet dress styles and moderate food-taking, it had not been a serene life. She had survived stressful periods filled with apprehension. She had refused an arranged marriage by her parents and eloped with this man who had only 20 kyats in hand at the time of elopement. But she never blamed him. She had tried her best to be a mature woman.

Because her husband did not take favours, he had not reached a higher position all along. But almost everyone showed him a deep and sincere respect and at gatherings, they treated him with great courtesy. Though she accepted it all but as a wife, she knew best that such principles were not too appropriate for long-term survival.

U Thaung Ngwe did not know that while he would be sitting in the living room with a guest and proudly reminiscing old times, his wife had to run and buy ten *ticals* of groundnut-oil and re-enter surreptitiously through the backdoor. He might not even have noticed that the plain green tea contained fewer and fewer tea leaves.

If she blurted it out, he would accuse her as a narrow-minded woman in front of other people. These days, he was more short-tempered. His had high blood pressure and, thus, she refrained from making him angry. In a family, if husband and wife were fighting frequently, the husband should realize that something was amiss.

While U Thaung Ngwe kept using exalting words for his principles, his peers had gained better positions and were doing well in life. He had previously kept a low profile but one of his chums saw him and reported, 'That man is facing a hard life with three kids.' So, he was offered a job at this department. Just as he said, he was offered the job because of what he had accomplished in the past, but was it not necessary to remind them of his existence?

Anyway, one should be grateful for a stable home and job. But income increment could not meet rising expenses. His principle was of no help and nobody bothered to help them anymore. Having said that, they were thankful that their status had not lessened. Daw Thin Kyi had to try on her own to make ends meet. Because of the husband's reproval, she could not work as a trader like the others. She dared not become a money-lender either. What Daw Thin Kyi knew was to economize expenses. The children were perplexed because of her thrifty ways.

Although she wanted to put meat curry in thick oil in the lunch boxes, she could just put a lot of vegetables fried with some meat. Soe Paing, the boy, could eat a lot and he loved meat curries. Although Yi Yi Mar did not say anything about her mother putting more meat in Soe Paing's lunch box, the middle one Ni Ni Mar pouted her lips. Daw Thin kyi had the habit of giving preference to males, and her excuse was 'he is a boy'.

Yi Yi Mar always made sacrifices.

The reason she kept repeating that she wanted to work was not out of youthful zest as her father thought but the mother knew why. Yi Yi Mar was beating around the bush so as not to annoy the father but Daw Thin Kyi just wanted to tell the reason outright to the husband.

After the eldest daughter Yi Yi Mar, there were the younger daughter Ni Ni Mar and the younger son Soe Paing. School expenses for the three of them was no joke. Trying to survive on his monthly salary of 500 kyats was telling on them and their situation was cognizable even from afar.

Why Yi Yi Mar wanted to work as a lower division clerk was quite apparent. Sometimes Daw Thin Kyi wondered if her husband pretended not to know. But that was not possible. Just by looking at the small flat they were lucky enough to live in made it evident. Even someone who did not want to acknowledge it could see it daily with their own eyes. The furniture in the flat was old and worn-out.

Daw Thin Kyi could no longer make beef curry and mutton tripe once a week for her husband who would say under pretence, 'I am getting old so I do not feel like eating meat curries. Instead, eating a lot of vegetables is good for digestion.' But if the wife went to the bazaar at noon, bought the meat at low price and cooked it for him after cleaning out the fatty bits, he would eat the dish with relish.

That was why Daw Thin Kyi thought that the father was not completely oblivious of why his daughter wanted to work.

From the outside, it would seem that young girls like Yi Yi Mar are easy-going and carefree. They were girls who went about boldly, spoke openly, and acted briskly. That was not, as her father put it, due to modern times. The times and environs necessitated one to be quick and alert in order to be recognized.

Last year, Yi Yi Mar failed the matric examination.

But you could not blame her. She studied hard but just before the exam, one department opened the post for clerical staff, so she took the job exam. If she got a job right after she passed the matriculation examination, she could take university correspondence courses.

But things did not happen as she had hoped for. With her eagerness for a job, Yi Yi Mar went here and there so she could not concentrate on her studies and, thus, failed the exam. She did not get the job either. Yi Yi Mar was deeply distressed. Now she had taken another exam for a job. She would take private tuition to sit for the matric exam again. It was absolutely imperative that Yi Yi Mar got a job.

The problem was her father.

She did not want to accuse her father of being an obsolete old man but she wanted to tell him that in certain situations, things had changed completely. In her father's times, not taking advantage was a dignified characteristic. She had listened to her father reminiscing about old times and their beliefs, so she understood moderately. Now, she was pleading with her father to ask for a favour, not to enrich himself but help his daughter get a job—and, as her father put it, for the country but first of all to make a living. She wanted her father to understand this much.

It was a situation where if nothing was done or said, nothing would come of it.

Father and his friends still held on to their old beliefs. It was good to hear these things when they gathered together and spoke with each other, but when they spoke among others, they were just be taken as squares. They could not see others wrinkling their nose at them. Even mother would now slyly tilt her chin and react with a grimace.

Some help from her father would satisfy Yi Yi Mar.

Father would not need to say much. Just a phone call and a few words about the daughter. Nothing more. If more needed to be said, father would be hesitant thinking it was like asking for favours. Some officers like to be approached for favours. If father thought the relevant person was not worth approaching, he would never do it. And he should not be sent to certain places. He would comment 'This man? Well, I know him. He was once an opportunist. He is the kind who gives little but expects much more in return.'

Yi Yi Mar did not gain her experiences casually. She got it by going in and out of offices and meeting with a lot of people in order to get a job.

Now, for the first time her father was compliant, so she expected an agreeable outcome.

* * *

Yi Yi Mar already had the practice of going to various offices, unflustered. She now entered this office and boldly went in to see the person she wanted to meet. She had found out who was the bigwig for this job, and her father had already given her the support she wanted.

'Father, do not say anything else. Just say that your daughter has applied for the post at that office,' she instructed her father.

The officer was a busy person so she could not enter directly. She had to sit and wait outside on a bench. There were three persons before her. If father knew, he would inappropriately comment 'Hmm, now only he is acting high and mighty!' That was why she came out today without her father's knowledge. Mother also did not want father to know.

One adult came out of the room. His appearance was posh and civil. Looking at the way he was strutting past, you could see he had got what he wanted.

The office help made a sign to another one waiting to go in. A fat lady went into the room lethargically. She held her big leather bag on her waist. It seemed she would take some time. Yi Yi Mar pitied the officer who was obliged to see one person after another. If it was her father, he would holler at those persons who came to plague him. That was also why he was not in this kind of position.

It was half an hour after the fat lady went in. What was she saying? She looked important. An office clerk came out and was seen bringing tea into the room. Taking tea and talking would take some time. At that time, a young girl arrived. She looked about the same age as Yi Yi Mar. But her dressing style was posh and she was wearing makeup. She sat beside Yi Yi Mar.

'Is Uncle in?' The girl asked Yi Yi Mar.

'Yes, he is,' Yi Yi Mar replied accommodatingly.

'Uncle is always busy. The last time I came. I had no chance to see him.' The girl complained. But though it was a complaint, she made it apparent, with satisfaction, that she was friendly with the officer in the room.

'An elderly lady has been in the room for some time,' Yi Yi Mar told her.

The girl was her own age group so Yi Yi Mar could keep company with her. She wondered if the girl had the same reason as her in coming here. But Yi Yi Mar realized that in experience as well as in sociability, the girl was way ahead of her.

'Such a lot of people plaguing uncle. I have also come to plague him.'

The girl was saying it proudly. Yes, she must be one of the applicants for the same job. Yi Yi Mar felt dispirited. 'In my case, father just knows this man. In her case, she herself is friendly with the man', she thought to herself and felt disheartened.

'Have you applied for a job?', Yi Yi Mar ventured to ask. The girl coolly nodded her head.

'I have applied for many jobs but none has come out well. With a college degree, instead of just lazing around, I would like to take up a job. So, I will take whatever job I can get. That is what I am going to tell uncle. At first, uncle had told me not to work in his department but that he would get me a job in another department.'

The girl said it boastingly. 'Oh, she is a graduate, is she?' Yi Yi Mar said in her mind. She herself had not even passed the matric exam. She felt like getting up and running away. The girl turned to her and asked.

'Have you applied for a job?'

Yi Yi Mar nodded her head and said dejectedly, 'But I do not think I will get it.'

Though the girl appeared to be fond of boasting, she seemed to have compassion for others. 'You cannot say. You may get it. Uncle is a generous person.'

Because of her encouragement, Yi Yi Mar was heartened. And there was father, too. If father said the man had a high regard for him, her attempt might succeed.

The elderly lady came out. Right up to the door, she did not stop talking. Even after pushing the swing- door, she again went in again and continued talking. 'I will come visit your house later. I would like to see Ma Khin Myint too.'

Finally, when the lady had left, Yi Yi Mar looked at the boy clerk and smiled quizzically at him.

'You may go in now.'

Yi Yi Mar smiled at the girl beside her and pulled open the swing door to enter. Her legs were somewhat trembling. A dignified gentleman was sitting at the table. On the table were the necessary office stationery and two telephones.

Yi Yi Mar stood humbly before the table. 'Well, say it. What are you here for?' The way the man spoke to her was not stern but full of authority. It also conveyed the message that she should speak briefly and to the point.

The boy clerk entered the room and took away the two coffee cups.

'I have applied for a job here at this office, Uncle. I am U Thaung Ngwe's daughter.' She mentioned her father's name in desperation.

'Oh, okay, sit down.'

Yi Yi Mar could not make out if he had indeed forgotten to ask her to sit and did it only when she mentioned her father's name. In any case, she felt a bit relieved. Of the three chairs in a row, she sat on the last one.

'Is your father in good health?'

'Yes, he is, Uncle.'

At least he asked about her father, Yi Yi Mar thought. In her mind, she heard her father saying 'Did not I tell you?'

'You have passed the written exam, have you not?'

'Yes, Uncle.'

'In which interview group are you?'

Yi Yi Mar's heart beat with trepidation and she thought this was a good sign. Perhaps, she would get the job this time. 'In the second group, Uncle.'

'Well, study what you have to. You know what to study, do you not? General knowledge about the work.'

'Yes, Uncle. Thank you very much. Father does not want me to work yet but I am enthusiastic about it.'

'Hmm, you will get a job. If you do not get this job, you will get another one.'

Not giving any definite assurance was the habit of elderly persons, Yi Yi Mar understood. But she was joyous just to be on the cards.

Yi Yi Mar wrote down her name and roll number on a sheet of paper and gave it to him with respect; then, she thanked him heartily. Upon coming out, she worried in case he had not taken the paper for safe keeping so she turned and looked back. The sheet of paper was still on the table. She prayed the swinging fan air would not blow it away.

* * *

'This Mya Pe is a useless person!'

Father was furious. He was often furious so it was nothing new but this time, it was important for Yi Yi Mar. Father being furious with this person called U Mya Pe could ruin her prospect of getting a job.

'If you do not want to say it, do not, Father. If I do not get this job, I will look for another one.'

Yi Yi Mar begged father. Otherwise, it would be awkward if he went and called Mya Pe a useless person. If she could not rely on father, she would find her own way. The date for interview was drawing near. If she got this job, everything would be fine as she expected. At the least, she would not need to ask for tuition fees and clothing expenses from her mother. She would make sure she passed the matric examination. Afterwards, she would take correspondence classes and get a degree. There would be no need then to look for a job. She would be able to support herself. If father and mother had one less burden on themselves, would it not be fine?

'My daughter should not be approaching him in a state of inferiority. I have never had a high regard for him. He is an opportunist.'

Father sometimes criticized other people like that. If a person did not conform to his principles, no matter what rank or position the person had, he did not think highly of him. His ruler was not for grade or rank but for principles. That was why some people were scared of father. They avoided him. And so, father was like an eccentric with non-conformist ideas. He did not realize that. Only Yi Yi Mar saw it.

'I will not, Father. I am just asking you if you know him.'

Yi Yi Mar tactfully diverted the topic. Otherwise, if she got the job, father would guess she had got it by approaching the person he did not like and would be furious. Oh, father! What an artless, straightforward, and simple father!

Meanwhile Yi Yi Mar's mother connived against her husband and advised her daughter behind his back.

'Do not tell your father everything. Do what you have to do. I made some enquiries. This department has promotion opportunities. Once you have a degree, you will get over 300 kyats. Getting a job is no small feat. Your father does not realize it.'

'I am aware of it, Mother. You yourself, Mother, do not go and tell father or he will find out.' Mother and daughter were conspiratorial.

When Yi Yi Mar received the appointment letter, she dared not tell her father immediately. She watched father's temperament and only when he was in a good mood, she told him. Luckily, he did not blame her.

Yi Yi Mar and her mother, even before she had started work, were looking forward with expectation to her pay day.

* * *

Yi Yi Mar did not feel sorry that she had to struggle early in life because there were plenty of girls her age working already. It was not strange that in offices all around Yangon, teenage girls were moving about animatedly. Some were in worse circumstances than Yi Yi Mar. Some were in better.

Once Yi Yi Mar started working, she had to spend over 100 kyats on two sets of uniform. But she was thankful for the uniform regulation. Otherwise, there would be undesirable clothing expenses. Even then, some girl clerks dressed up smarter than others. Yi Yi Mar could not comprehend how they could afford to do it.

As Yi Yi Mar now had a job, in the morning, in addition to the fried rice mother usually prepared for father, she put more ingredients and cooked for the whole family. Yi Yi Mar's lunch box was nothing extraordinary, just vegetables mixed with meat. But since mother put more meat for both the younger son and Yi Yi Mar, the older woman had less to eat.

Yi Yi Mar could not afford to buy a new basket so like some girls she slung her leather bag over her shoulder and held the lunch box in her hand. How nice it would be if the office were within walking distance, even though Yi Yi Mar did not mind walking—no matter how far. She did not want to ride the bus, but since the ferry bus was not yet available, she had to take the bus. Luckily, her office was on a different road from her father's. Sometimes, an office car came to pick up father as an officer from his office lived nearby.

Considering the waiting time at the bus stop and the time on the bus, Yi Yi Mar had to start an hour ahead of her office time. By the time she arrived at the office, it was 9.30 a.m. Being a new staff, she needed to be punctual. Thwet Thwet Aye, the girl she had met at the officer uncle's office, was posted to the same branch as hers. She came from U Wisara road in a Mazda car. Both girls wanted a job but their circumstances were not the same. But Yi Yi Mar's placidity ensured that she got along with everyone. Since she secured a job before passing the matric examination, nobody bothered to make gestures of disapproval.

Once she got to the office, she had to sign in the attendance register, go to her seat, dust the chair and desk, seat herself, and regain her breath. And then she had to greet the other staff around her.

'Mi Shwe Mar, what curry do you have?' The typist girl seated beside her asked Yi Yi Mar. It was the only question she could be asked. In no time, elder female clerks who liked to talk about their children and Daw Than Kyi who brought shoes to the office to sell with monthly instalment would be arriving. The office room would be alive with a teeming crowd. And when branch clerk Ko Than Tin, who enjoyed talking about filthy topics cloaked in funny words, arrived, everyone will be shouting and jostling each other.

'It is pot herb fried with prawn Ma Ma Aye, you can share.' Yi Yi Mar's curries were better than Ma Aye who usually fried roselle leaves or soap acacia with the right amount of fish paste and did not add any dried prawn. But her spicy and sour curries were delicious so no one was hesitant to exchange their curry for hers.

'Oh, good. A person who can eat pot herb at this early season is a wealthy person!' Yi Yi Mar smiled in her mind at Ma Aye's words. Mother was adept in such matters. In the jengkol season too, mother bought them first. Her bazaar time was not in the early hours like other housewives. Mostly it was after 11 a.m. when the sellers were beginning to disperse. By then, the sellers who had to get up in the wee hours would be getting drowsy and preparing for nap after their meal.

It was at this time that mother would enter the bazaar. The sellers who were preparing to leave, sold their vegetables at bargain prices. In the wet market too, while they were washing their baskets and bowls, they would sell the remaining pieces of meat cheaply. Some did not even use the pair of scales. They simply weighed by hand.

Nobody was any wiser about this. Even father might not have a full idea. Father sometimes praised mother for managing his salary meticulously but it was doubtful he knew how she was actually managing it.

Now, because Yi Yi Mar got a job, mother was in debt!

Daw Thin Kyi needed money to make clothes and buy shoes for the daughter, so she went and borrowed money from her elder sister, whom she usually plagued when she was in need. Her elder sister was not an officer's wife like her. Her husband was not a notable person either. He was an ordinary seller. He sold fruits at the Keighley market. They were in comfortable circumstances. They had no pretence. Both were simple and honest. Although mother had to borrow money from them, her sister had respect for mother and her husband, and also treated father with respect.

By this time, almost all the staff had arrived.

Thwet Thwet Aye, wearing a white jacket of novel design and good material and a new longyi together with a pair of white high-heeled shoes, entered the room vividly with springy steps. Thwet Thwet Aye could afford to be vivid. Her father was a senior government officer but she did not work in her father's department. She chose to work here. At first, Yi Yi Mar could not understand why but later she comprehended. There were complicated elements of give-and-take and mutual exchanges.

She dared not talk about this to her father. Moreover, she did not want her father to know that the office she was working in was under U Mya Pe. But one day, father was sure to find out and Yi Yi Mar had no idea how to face that situation.

Thwet Thwet Aye threw down her pretty leather bag onto her desk. Brushing the hair on her neck with one hand, she walked to the table where the attendance register was. Branch clerk U Sein Chit handed her the ball point pen. Yi Yi Mar had heard of people who flattered the seniors and suppressed the juniors but never seen them. She guessed U Sein Chit was that kind of man. When girl typists and lower division girl clerks of lower circumstances were late just for about five minutes, U Sein Chit was ready to circle their name in red ink. But when a girl like Thwet Thwet Aye was late and gave an excuse such as 'the car broke down, U Sein Chit', he would chuckle baring his teeth.

Though having the same rank of lower division clerk and the same entry date, Yi Yi Mar and Thwet Thwet Aye did not have the same advantages. Thwet Thwet Aye was going to sit another exam conducted by the department and if she passed, she would be promoted. It was quite certain she would pass. Yi Yi Mar had no such prospect. She must pass matric exam this year to be more qualified.

Thwet Thwet Aye returned to her seat and sat down daintily. Then she turned to look at Yi Yi Mar and greeted her. Thwet Thwet Aye got to sit beside probationary officer Daw Kyin Yi and assistant officer Daw Yin Mya. Yi Yi Mar had to sit beside typist girls, Ma Aye and Ma Nge. But Thwet Thwet Aye knew how to fraternize with Yi Yi Mar and the rest. That was why even though they gossiped about her behind her back, in front of her they were all smiles.

As for Yi Yi Mar—perhaps she got this trait from her father—if she did not feel like it, she would not speak sweetly or smile. Therefore, Yi Yi Mar had fewer friends than Thwet Thwet Aye. Also, nobody knew who Yi Yi Mar's father was whereas the whole office knew that Thwet Thwet Aye's father was once a political colleague of the head of department. Therefore, Daw Kyin Yi and Daw Yin Mya tried to flatter Thwet Thwet at all times.

'Mar, please accompany me this afternoon.' Thwet Thwet came and propped her two hands on Yi Yi Mar's desk. If Thwet Thwet Aye wanted to go out during office hours, she asked only Yi Yi Mar to go along with her. Yi Yi Mar went with her out of delicacy although she feared she might be admonished for going out often after so short a service. Even if the others did not say anything, Yi Yi Mar herself wanted to fulfil her duties. She hated to take it easy. Yi Yi Mar believed that this was a quality she had inherited from her father. Father was too exacting and incisive at work, so everyone tilted their chin up at him as a square peg. Yi Yi Mar did not apply for a job at her father's office because she did not want to be in the same office as him. Her father himself never mentioned to her about getting a job at his office.

'Thwet, where are you going?' This time Yi Yi Mar thought of refusing to go with her.

'Just around the corner. To the clinic. I want to go and ask for some aspirin.' Thwet Thwet Aye winked at her almost unnoticeably and replied. Yi Yi Mar knew instantly. It was either to the Bogyoke Market or Open Air market, to buy jacket material or collect a jacket from the tailor.

'Perhaps Ma Ma Mya is free,' Yi Yi Mar said without committing herself. 'No, I do not want to go with old ladies. It will not take long, Mar.'

'Mar, go along with her. Or, do you want me to accompany you?' Ma Ma Aye who felt compelled, asked Thwet Thwet Aye.

'No. I am asking her because I am fond of her. This is one last time. I will not ask again.' Thwet Thwet Aye said it liltingly so Yi Yi Mar could no longer refuse.

This time she would go but next time she would refuse curtly, Yi Yi Mar thought to herself and got up from her seat. She gave Ma Aye the edited letters to type. Yi Yi Mar's job was to read and edit office letters. Just one step above the typist. Thwet Thwet Aye had to take care of office figures and such, but she was helped by office superintendent Ko Than Tin who had the habit of treating the female staff with familiarity. Although he gave an excuse that he was helping her out as she was a new recruit, those in the department who knew him laughed at him mockingly.

Yi Yi Mar accompanied Thwet Thwet Aye, but she was not too keen. This was especially because to go out, it was necessary to get the permission letter signed by U Mya Pe in his room. Yi Yi Mar hated to see U Mya Pe. If he made conversation before signing the letter, it would take about fifteen minutes. Thwet Thwet Aye herself was talkative.

At first when Yi Yi Mar met U Mya Pe, she had the opinion that his disposition was not as bad as father had put it. He had received Yi Yi Mar and her mother cordially and chatted about old times. He talked about going into politics in the past in his native town and then he laughed heartily.

'Of course, this much I have to help. How can I forget that at one time your house was our sanctuary,' he said frankly. 'In which department is my elder brother now?'

Mother told him the name of father's department and his rank. U Mya Pe looked surprised. 'It seems my brother is still a square peg like before?' U Mya Pe remarked.

'Yes, as usual.'

He laughed raucously.

'Your daughter resembles you, Sister.'

Yi Yi Mar did not like U Mya Pe's remark but she smiled anyway. Actually, Yi Yi Mar wanted to tell him that she was her father's daughter, that she had inherited more than half of her father's spirit. Looking at U Mya Pe's smiling face, she pondered that perhaps he was not as honest as the other uncle she had met previously.

It was nothing new that Yi Yi Mar was posted to this office. One would get posted according to one's connections. She understood before long that she would be somebody's subordinate. The place of work was a training ground for worldly wisdom. Whatever was in store, she would have to overcome. Her foremost intention was to relieve her mother of her expenses, and then for herself to go move in her future.

'Hey, these two girls, where are you going again?'

As soon as they entered the room, U Mya Pe asked familiarly. Thwet Thwet Aye approached his table boldly.

'My mother, Uncle. She is not well and she asked me to buy medicine from the Open-Air Market. She could have asked my father's office boys to buy for her but she insisted I do it.' Thwet Thwet Aye's reasons were full of guile and never monotonous.

'What about this girl?' He turned to Yi Yi Mar and asked with a smile. Yi Yi Mar did not like this man's smile from the very beginning. Now, her dislike had increased. She had heard about him through the grapevine of a thousand mouths in the office.

'My companion as usual, Boss. My mother has warned me about going out alone.'

U Mya Pe drew the letter towards him and instead of signing it, he made a phone call. He made a sign to them with one hand to wait awhile. Thwet Thwet Aye sat down leisurely and was turning the pages of a *Newsweek* magazine. Yi Yi Mar was impatient. When she had visited father's office once and there was a phone call, father had cut short his reply, she remembered.

'Ha ha ha, yes really? Of course, of course.' U Mya Pe was taking some time with the phone conversation. In the end, 'Right, right. Let us meet up one time.' He concluded and put down the mouthpiece gently.

Yi Yi Mar heaved a hidden sigh.

'Well, how is your mother? Is she in good health?'

He turned to Yi Yi Mar while signing the paper and asked her. Yi Yi Mar smiled accommodatingly and nodded her head. Since she got to this office, she had acquired the habit of smiling. What kind of smile, she herself could not tell. But it was not the right kind of smile, she knew for sure.

'You are sitting for the matric exam this year, are you not?'
'Yes, Uncle.'

'Which tuition are you attending?' 'I do not know yet, Uncle.'

'Hmm, after tuition fees and car fare, what is left of your salary?' Yi Yi Mar just smiled.

'It cannot be helped, Uncle. She is not the daughter of a well-paid senior officer like you.' Thwet Thwet Aye tilted her chin up and remarked.

'I am not as well-paid as your father, girl. Yi Yi Mar's father also has the ability to work in a much higher position than the current one but he is not keen, I suppose. Is it not so?'

Yi Yi Mar smiled again.

This time it was a genuine smile. She knew her father would never receive a high salary. It crossed her mind that if her father was in this man's place, he would not be talking too long on the phone about non-office matters. And he would not be chatting away with office girls.

Thwet Thwet Aye continued chatting. U Mya Pe was laughing with amusement. Yi Yi Mar tried to stop Thwet Thwet

Aye by reaching out and taking the signed paper. She started to get up. Only then did Thwet Thwet Aye get up too. The female clerks outside his room looked at the two of them coming out. For whatever reason they were looking, Yi Yi Mar felt embarrassed.

As usual, Thwet Thwet Aye went to the tailor. Yi Yi Mar was as angry as Thwet Thwet Aye with the defaulting tailor who never finished the jackets on time. If they had to keep coming time and again, would it not be troublesome? Yi Yi Mar felt somewhat relieved when she saw several office girls in uniform walking up and down Bogyoke Market.

After getting the jacket, Thwet Thwet Aye went around the market. After checking out the new clothing materials, Thwet Thwet Aye declared she would buy them after receiving her salary. All this had nothing to do with her, Yi Yi Mar felt. She was a young girl so, of course, she would like to buy pretty clothes for herself but when she thought of her mother sweating it out in the kitchen preparing meals for the family, her desire was curbed altogether. She thought of buying her mother some voile fabric after drawing her salary.

When they got back to the office, they had their lunch. After lunch, some females grouped around and chatted together. The high-pitched voice of Thwet Thwet Aye could be heard. Most of the staff enjoyed fawning around Thwet Thwet Aye who was beautiful, a graduate, and a senior officer's daughter. Her work concerned tracking leaves and managing salaries, so it was not pressing. As for Yi Yi Mar, she tried to get her work done as quickly as possible. And for that, some praised her but some criticized her saying she was working hard because she had a low level of education and she feared being sacked. So, she was trying to earn favour from the bosses.

Yi Yi Mar entering the workplace was so much like a small bird leaving the mother's bosom to suddenly fly into the big wide world.

* * *

If one said buses in Yangon were congested, it would be like saying there is water in the sea. It was nothing new. Although mother gave her an amount just a little over the bus fare, Yi Yi Mar pressed her little leather bag against her bosom. If her bag was cut open, she would have to buy another one. This had happened to some of the office some girls as well. Their leather bags had been cut open and since they could not afford to buy new ones, they just had them patched up. When there were plural patches, they jokingly named it 'centipede design'.

From the bus stop, Yi Yi Mar had to walk briskly to their flat. She had not much extra time. She climbed up to their room on the third floor in a hurry, threw down the lunch box and leather bag, and then drank a glass of water.

'The office clerk is back!' Her younger brother teased. Her younger sister's school was in the afternoon session so she was not back yet.

'Mother, what is there for dinner today?' Yi Yi Mar shouted into the kitchen and asked. Mother's situation was rather funny. She would not cook a variety of dishes but she could never get out of the kitchen. Sometimes she would say, 'Hey, cooking a meat curry in thick oil is quick and easy. Cutting the vegetables, preparing the fish paste, grinding the fermented soya-bean, and so on, all these require elaborate steps.'

At home, they had to rely on fermented bean paste, fermented soya-bean and fish paste curry. These dishes, although without meat, were appetizing. Since her father suffered from hypertension, mother cooked cezana leaf soup and all of them joined in and drank the saltless soup.

'Today, it is tenderized butter beans and concinna leaves. You may eat it with salted mango pickle before you go.'

Yi Yi Mar wrinkled her nose behind her mother's back. Mother and father both liked butter beans as they hailed from upcountry but Yi Yi Mar did not find it tasty. At least in upcountry, they cooked with an adequate number of plums and it tasted better.

'I will eat when I get back. When your younger daughter comes back, tell her to wait for me to eat together.' Yi Yi Mar thought that instead of eating alone now, it would be more enjoyable to eat with her sibling after returning from her tuition class.

Yi Yi Mar changed from her office uniform to casual clothes and went out with her cloth sling bag. Wearing a plain tetoron longyi and a closed pattern check blouse, she felt light and nimble. Although she had to lead the younger ones as she was the eldest, Daw Thin Kyi often gazed at her youthful daughter with compassion. Now, she had no time to glance at Yi Yi Mar because she was preparing a delicious fish paste sauce.

Yi Yi Mar ran down the stairs swiftly. She bought a banana for 30 pyas at the betel shop at the top of the road and ate it while walking. When she got to the tuition class, she first drank a glass of water.

It was not a well-renowned tuition but the teacher was benevolent. He was the son of a middle-class officer and a graduate. Reasoning that it was more of a hobby than a source of extra income, he had started the tuition class with only about ten students. Although he did not entertain them with jokes like at other tuitions, he explained the lessons with patience so Yi Yi Mar and the other students found him agreeable.

'What is wrong, drinking such a lot of water?' Naung Naung was always watching Yi Yi Mar. He lived one apartment away from Yi Yi Mar's. If she met him alone, he was quiet and friendly but when he was with friends, he cracked jokes quite boldly.

'I am thirsty, that is why.' Yi Yi Mar went and sat in the front row. The classroom, partitioned from the frontage, was not too spacious. Naung Naung sat behind Yi Yi Mar.

'Yi Yi Mar, I heard you are already working, are you?'

Some students had not yet arrived. Yi Yi Mar took out an exercise book and read from it. 'Hey, did you not hear me ask you a question?'

'Oh, yes.'

'Why do you work? Even without working, you failed the exam.'

Naung Naung was comparing with himself in saying like this. His father had quite a high salary and he was the only son. But he had been taking the matric exam for three years. At the tea shop at the top of the road or at the staircases, Naung Naung and friends could be seen playing the guitar or just sitting around.

Yi Yi Mar gave a curt reply. Other girls arrived. 'It cannot be helped if I fail!'

'I am saying this because I pity to see you work.' Naung Naung said closely to her ears. She had been friendly with him because they lived in the same quarter but these days his behaviour was getting bold and Yi Yi Mar was exasperated.

'Naung Naung, if you sit behind me, be quiet. Do not be talkative. I cannot hear the teacher.'

The small room was full of students now. The teacher who must have rested awhile after getting back from the office entered the room.

The teacher solved and explained Maths problems that he thought important for three- or four-time repeaters. Yi Yi Mar had no chance to rest at the office today. She was tired from going around Bogyoke Market. And, she was hungry too. The teacher's voice was low, and Naung Naung was whispering from behind about she knew not what. Fatigue overwhelmed her and she became drowsy.

But with the determination that this year she must pass the matric exam, she tried her best to keep her eyes and ears open.

* * *

'I am warning you because I am fond of you. Do not take it badly,' Ma Ma Aye told her.

'I will not Ma Ma Aye, I will not .'

Yi Yi Mar heaved a sigh furtively. The problem was, Thwet Thwet Aye never went out alone. And she had a lot of reasons and places to go to. Going out was one thing. Going into that room without any apparent reason was the problem. And whenever she went, she poked Yi Yi Mar and asked her to come along. Once inside the room, instead of talking about office matters, they talked about trivial things. U Mya Pe had the body and looks most fair girls found attractive. He looked younger than his age. It was office gossip that he was not in good terms with his wife.

'That is deliberate advertisement!' Ma Ma Aye whispered.

'I am in a fix Ma Ma Aye. He calls me often to edit letters. If he does not call, Thwet Thwet Aye calls me to join her when she goes to that room. We are new girls so others are sure to criticize.'

'Others dare not criticize her because of her influence.' Ma Ma Aye continued hesitantly.

Yi Yi Mar understood what Ma Ma Aye was implying. There is a tendency to kick a person when they are down. Yi Yi

Mar was not someone to use her father's influence. Her father's rank and position were not one of influence but if his name was mentioned, one could be sure that he would be honoured and respected.

'I thought at first that if I worked, I would get to learn about office matters and that I would have personal income. That was all I had in mind but now I find that there are such a lot of other things to learn. But once I get home, there is no time to ponder about all this. After going to tuition class and learning my lessons, I get so tired. I just fall asleep with a book in my hand.'

Ma Ma Aye smiled genially. 'I recognize your integrity, Yi Yi Mar. Of the new recruits in this section, you are young but you have mature thinking. Some fail to appreciate it. They just assess superficially and look down their nose.'

'Thank you, Ma Ma Aye. Rather than trying to escape criticism, I will try to behave properly on my own account.' Yi Yi Mar said, and in a hushed tone, said to herself, 'Saying this is easy . . . '

Having to start confronting life's implications, was it not a bit too early?

* * *

'I want to work too, Mother.'

Everyone looked at Ni Ni Mar. She was acting serious and did not glance at anyone. Mother had a mouthful of rice in her hand but she did not put it in her mouth and instead looked at Ni Ni Mar in amazement.

Everyone in the family knew Ni Ni Mar was headstrong and had a childish attitude. If she was dissatisfied with something, instead of talking about it at first would act grudgingly or quiet down. If nobody took action, she would disclose her dissatisfaction one way or another.

Now what Ni Ni Mar had said showed that there was something she had a grudge against. She was only in eighth standard. How could she qualify for a job?

'What kind of work do you want to do? I heard they are hiring charwomen at father's office!' Soe Paing loved to tease. Ni Ni Mar did not smile but cast a glance at her younger brother through the corner of her eye.

'I will work even if I get a cleaning job. In the family, I lose face for not having a job. Father praises one who works. Mother favours one who works.'

Mother's face fell. Yi Yi Mar wanted to scold her younger sister for being so unaware of their existing circumstances and hurting her mother's feelings. But she remembered that Ni Ni Mar usually forgot everything once she had aired her dissatisfaction so Yi Yi Mar refrained from saying anything.

'What kind of favouritism am I accorded? You mean to say you have less curry in your lunch box?'

'That one is repetitive! I am tired of hearing the same things over and over,' Mother clawed at Yi Yi Mar to stay silent. Ni Ni Mar got up from the dinner table grudgingly. She had shown her dissatisfaction. The case was closed.

'What is wrong with your daughter?' Yi Yi Mar asked her mother in a low voice.

'She wanted a new schoolbag. I told her the one she has now is still new and that I cannot afford to buy her a new bag every year.'

Yi Yi Mar knew right away. From her salary, mother had bought a pretty new basket for her as she was anxious that riding the bus while holding onto the lunch box might be inconvenient for her daughter.

'Buy a new bag for her, Mother. Keep the old one for Soe Paing. The boy is happy so long as he gets enough to eat!'

'Never mind, never mind. Instead of buying a new bag for her, I will buy 1 viss of pork meat and cook it deliciously for all to eat!'

Yi Yi Mar now realized how invaluable family life was, especially the free talk between siblings. Spending a carefree life among family members was a lot more pleasant than moving in the office circle. But to solve family problem, one was obliged to get a job. But now she had learnt to leave office matters at the office and keep home and family matters at home.

'Has not father come back yet, Mother?'

'He told me he would be dropping in to see his chums. Of course, they would talk and reminisce as usual.'

'Let him talk, Mother. At first I thought father was being extreme but now I realize most of what he said is all true.'

The two younger ones were no longer around so mother and daughter were left alone in the kitchen. As Yi Yi Mar was the eldest daughter, her mother consulted with her in all matters.

'What is all true, tell me.' Mother asked while she washed the plates.

Yi Yi Mar placed the plates on the rack and pondered how to make her mother understand her feelings. Mother was always wrinkling her nose at father but Yi Yi Mar came to realize that in actuality, mother did not look down on her husband. At one time, had she not turned against everyone and married father?

'What father always says about errant officers.'

'Oh.' Mother glanced at Yi Yi Mar who was talking high and mighty.

'Yes, Mother. Previously, I thought father was being a square and criticizing other people. Now I realize why he says such words.'

Mother was not dense. She nodded her head in agreement with Yi Yi Mar's words. At the same time, there showed on her face a concern for her daughter.

'In whatever situation you are, behave accordingly, Daughter. Do not just tell others snidely that you are in the right and cannot be bothered. Sometimes, you need to prove that you are above reproach.'

'Yes, Mother.'

Mother and daughter both knew what they were talking about.

'You are too young yet to be working. When you pass the matric, stop working. Just go to the university and study.' Mother's anxiety was growing.

'I will not quit, Mother. Later I will have to work anyway. Now that I am working in advance, I am getting experience. Do not be anxious for me, Mother.'

Mother had a vacant look. Then she said in a whisper. 'Do not talk about office matters in front of your father, Daughter.'

* * *

'Thwet said she requested your company because she was fond of you but now, she has no idea why you are avoiding her. She said she is not a girl of loose character that you are acting in this way.' Yi Yi Mar heard Thwet Thwet Aye's bitter words from another staff. Yi Yi Mar's rational behaviour had deteriorated her friendship with Thwet Thwet Aye. For this, she was sorry. Thwet Thwet Aye was a friendly person. Yi Yi Mar tried to think of a way to explain the misunderstanding but she found none.

Office gossip was spreading. The exaggerated words were shameful to hear. Yi Yi Mar was lucky to have evaded the situation. It was shameful; it was sad. As her mother had mentioned, if she was in the right, she should not be bothered, but for a youthful and delicate girl like Yi Yi Mar, these words were too harsh.

Thwet Thwet Aye waived the gossip as unimportant. With sarcasm for Yi Yi Mar, she went about alone. She entered and exited where she wished and as she wished. There is a Myanmar idiom that says if a snail imitates a frog and tries to jump, its own pool of water will be destroyed. Yi Yi Mar dared not imitate the frog and had no desire for it either. She was only concerned with subsidizing her mother's bazaar money, buying a new schoolbag for her younger sister, and feeding her younger brother plenty of meat dishes.

She was going in circles between home and office and tuition.

When exams drew near, she had to take leave from work. The usual tuition was not enough. She was tired out from attending special classes and studying special notes. Meanwhile, father suffered from hypertension and mother told him she thought that he should retire from work. Father could no longer speak in a loud voice like before. For the first time, he aired his anxiety, 'If I retire, how would you all survive?'

Mother replied hesitantly. 'Ma Win is asking me to join her. She said I would have to do nothing tiring. Just to stay beside her and help her.'

Ma Win was mother's elder sister. Perhaps she was asking mother to be a seller. Father no longer shouted at mother in anger. He seemed to have become lenient and considerate.

'If my children can stand on their own feet before I pass away, you will have no cause for anxiety. That is why I teach my children the important things in life, especially how to nurture their spirit. Youth must have a high spirit. They must work. They must work harder than in our times. Times have changed and population has increased, cost of living has increased, living space has become scarce, so it is natural for everyone to feel the pinch. But if for that reason, someone takes advantage of his situation with the family's welfare in mind, that person is a no-hoper. However, much he gets to live in wealthy circumstances, it is meaningless.'

Mother began to look away. To mother who had been with father for so long, his words must be clichéd.

Father was tired. But he was satisfied only if he had his say no matter how tired he was. Yi Yi Mar had to show interest in his words.

'Perhaps I am not notable in terms of rank and financial status, but I have lived my life as an invaluable and dutiful countryman not taking advantage of opportunities. I want it to be acknowledged by my children. And I want all my children to be like that.' Father's voice became low-pitched. Yi Yi Mar looked at him with pride. Though most people regarded him as a square person, Yi Yi Mar did not think so. Father had worked with benevolence for the post he was accorded. By comparing her father with the officers she now knew, Yi Yi Mar began to respect her father even more.

* * *

Yi Yi Mar tried to do her best in the exam. Because all three children had their exams, mother was tired out. She went to the bazaar much later than usual. Cooking hours in the kitchen also took longer than usual. Their dinner table had an added variety of dishes. Yi Yi Mar knew that mother was sneaking off to her elder sister without father's knowledge.

Yi Yi Mar tried to forget everything during the exam. For her, this exam counted as a life exam. On the first day she went back to office after the exam, she heard the latest news. U Mya Pe had been transferred to another department. He did what he wanted in his own interest and had paved his own way up.

Thwet Thwet Aye had taken an exam for a probationary officer post and had passed it. The last piece of news was supposed to be good for Yi Yi Mar. She was to be a trainee for a departmental refresher course and after that she would be eligible for promotion and might move to another section.

Yi Yi Mar was not discouraged. She decided to do her best. She was sure she would pass the matric exam. Her future was clear. The refresher course would be enjoyable. It would open new doors. But she wondered where she might be posted. Mother would be anxious if she knew. Supposing she got transferred to another district, it would be problematic.

Yi Yi Mar did not worry for herself. She worried for mother. She was mother's comfort and consolation. The moon has its own illumination, but is it not better to have a revolving star that is bright and shining?

At home, if only father's leadership, mother's management, and Yi Yi Mar's effort were maintained and upheld, it would serve the family better, especially for the two younger siblings. All three children would then be able to follow father's footsteps. Yi Yi Mar had the greatest respect for her father who had laid down sacred principles for the children to adhere to.

Her father had in no way caused shame to the family. Yi Yi Mar made a resolution that their father would have no cause to feel shame because of his children. Let him remain in good health until all his children could stand on their own feet. Yi Yi Mar braced herself with her father's words in mind. 'People must work for their country. The country must take responsibility for its people. Otherwise . . . '

Bearing the latest office news with her, Yi Yi Mar pushed and shoved her way into the bus and took the ride home to the family haven.

June 1982

Chronological Record of the Author's Biography and Literary Works

24 October 1944: Born in Daik-U town to parents, U Tun and Daw Mya Shin, and named San San

1952: Started school at Daik-U Government High School

1956: Won a fourth standard scholarship

1959: Started writing poems in seventh standard; worked as executive member of the school library and wall journal committees

1960–1964: Won district essay contests as a high school student

1964: Passed matriculation examination

1965: Started university as Maths major student at the Rangoon Arts and Science University

March 1965: Wrote her first poem *Ywet Hla Pann Lay Koe Bawa* in *Taing Yin May* journal

January–November 1968: Worked as a primary school teacher at Primary School No. 23 in North Okkalapa township

6 November 1969: Married U Myo Nyunt (Sarpay Lawka)

May 1970: Wrote her first article *Pyin Sin Chel Tha Myet Lone Ah-hla* in *Taing Yin May* journal

147

September 1972: Wrote her first short story *Ain Nee Chin* in *Ngwe Tar Yi* magazine

1972–1978: Worked as assistant research officer at the Burma Socialist Program Party Research branch

October 1974: Wrote her first full-length novel *Pyaut Thaw Lann Hmar Sann Ta Warr*. This novel won her the 1974 National Literary Award

February 1975: Wrote *Pwint Tachoet, Kyway Tachoet*

August 1975: Wrote *Ywet Hla Pann*

May 1976: Wrote the story *Ngapali*

October 1976: Wrote *Achit Hso Thaw Ayar*

May 1977: Wrote *Bel Thu Lar Ku Ba Mel*

April 1978: Wrote *Hma Tabar Achar Mashi Byi*

July 1978: Wrote *Thatbay Thattar Awayyar Hawntu*

November 1978: Wrote *Hma Ta Sint*

1978: Published *Pyaut Thaw Lann Hmar Sann Ta Warr* in Russian

August 1979: Wrote *Shwedagon Go Myin Hlyin*

December 1979: Wrote *Ma Nyein Go Shet Par*

April 1980: Wrote *Joe*

June 1980: Published *Magazine Full-length Stories*, which won the 1980 National Literary Award for Collected Short Stories

October 1980: Wrote *Thamuddaya Khunasinn, Myit Minn Taset Thone Thwe*

1980: Published *Bel Thu Lar Ku Ba Mel* in Russian

February 1981: Wrote *Kyway Malo Net Wai, Wai Malo Net Kyway*

October 1981: Wrote *Pann Yaing Tayar*

December 1981: Wrote *Nyi Ma Lay Ga Achit Ko Koe Kwe Thadet Larr*

February 1982: Wrote *Ma Thudamma Sar Yi*

May 1982: Published *Short Stories Volume 1*, which won the 1982 National Literary Award for Collected Short Stories

September 1982: Wrote *Waidanar Kyarni Pwint*

December 1982: Wrote *Thone Loon Tin Hma Kyo*

1982: Published *Hma Tabarr Achar Mashit Byi* and *Pyaut Thaw Lann Hmar Sann Tawarr* in Japanese

June 1983: Wrote *Manar Makyann Thi Oh Hninsi*

August 1983: Wrote *Myanmar Pyi Hmar Nay Gya Thi* and *Kyway Yin Ahtutu Kyway Mel*

June 1985: Wrote *Mee Yaung Out Ko Win Hlyin*

October 1985: Wrote *Myittar Kannar Achit Thit Pin*

December 1985: Published *Hto Nayt Ga Mee Malar Bar* and *Moe Moe Inya's Full-length Stories*

July 1986: Published *Moe Moe Inya's Short Stories Volume 2*, which won the 1986 National Literary Award for Collected Short Stories

April 1987: Wrote *Khatet Nu Kalay Tway Hnyo Chain Tan Tot*

1988: The story *Sagar Maso Wunt Aung* was translated into English and featured in the *Lotus* magazine published by the Afro-Asian Writers Association

August 1989: The short story *Ain Nee Chin* was translated into Japanese and featured in the women's magazine, *Fujinno Tomo*

August 1989–March 1990: Worked as Executive Editor for *Sabei Pyu* magazine

13 March 1990: Died